THE NO NAME GANG

They were ruthless homicidal outlaws, but anonymous, so the New Mexico law authorities were frustrated. The No Name Gang murdered and looted and got away every time. But in a ghost town called Midas Mound, justice awaited the elusive desperadoes. Two drifters were in seclusion there, and their names were Valentine and Emerson. When it came to the final reckoning, the Texas Trouble-Shooters were outnumbered, but their foes were outclassed.

MARSHALL GROVER

THE NO NAME GANG

A Larry & Stretch Western

Complete and Unabridged

LINFORD
Leicester

First published by
Horwitz Grahame Pty Limited
Australia

First Linford Edition
published 1997
by arrangement with
Horwitz Publications Pty Limited
Australia

British Library CIP Data

Grover, Marshall
    Larry & Stretch: the no name gang.
    —Large print ed.—Linford western library
    1. Western stories, Australian
    2. Large type books
    I. Title II. Larry & Stretch
    823 [F]

    ISBN 0-7089-5088-4

Published by
F. A. Thorpe (Publishing) Ltd.
Anstey, Leicestershire

Set by Words & Graphics Ltd.
Anstey, Leicestershire
Printed and bound in Great Britain by
T. J. International Ltd., Padstow, Cornwall

This book is printed on acid-free paper

1

After the Storm

WHEN the storm hit Quimera, New Mexico, the night of July 1st, the local administration naturally hoped it would be of short duration. If the downpour persisted another three days, as had been known to happen, the town's 4th of July festivities would be a shambles. Fortunately, the streets were not yet bedecked by bunting to be saturated by the rain transforming the main thoroughfare to a quagmire.

The lightning flashes were day-bright, the thunder deafening. By 1.30 a.m., the town was closed down, the only local out and about a patrolling deputy, Mike Harrow, working the graveyard shift and cursing his luck; predictably, Harrow did more sheltering than patrolling, retreating into doorways or shivering under awnings in his dripping slicker, craving the comfort of his bed. He was a full four blocks away from the Merchant's National Bank when its rear door was blasted open, its safe also, and $75,000 seized.

It would be remarked later that the robbers had everything going for them. For bank bandits, conditions could not have been better. Both blasts were well and truly muffled, coinciding with thunder-claps, so the deputy was none the wiser.

The storm had begun around noon. It was 4.45 a.m. of the 2nd when the downpour eased a little and Harrow became mobile again. His patrol took him four blocks downtown and, upon discovering the bank's street windows had been shattered, he cocked his shotgun and trudged the muddy side alley to the rear of the building.

Ten minutes later he was rousing his boss. The sheriff of Quimera County, Ritchie Winters, did all that could be reasonably expected. Other men rose early that morning, a hardy eight always available to be deputized when a posse was needed.

But, by noon of July 2nd, when the Winters posse sighted Fortuna Pass, the sheriff knew the bank robbers had won. They had time on their side as well as the weather, must have travelled through the pass hours ago, and the pass marked the west border of Quimera County; Winters could pursue no farther.

He had led this posse with his other deputy, Eli Blain, siding him.

"They got away with it," Blain said sourly, after his boss ordered a return to the county seat. "All eight of the cunning bastards."

"You figure eight?" prodded Winters.

"Horse tracks were hard to calculate, what with the trail all muddied up," shrugged Blain. "But I figure eight at least."

"The hell of it is they had it all their own way," Winters said bitterly. "Thunder so loud the dynamite couldn't be heard, plenty time for the getaway, the storm — everything."

"You had Mike wire the San Raphael law before we deputed our friends," said Blain. "That's as much as you could do."

"It still sticks in my craw," complained Winters.

He was still disgruntled 8 o'clock the morning of July 3rd, slumped in a caneback placed by the outer rail of his office porch. The storm had passed. Steam rose from puddles along Main Street, the sun shone bright and gaily-painted banners and bunting had been strung. The street looked a lot cheerier than Winters felt when Lorin Powell climbed the steps, planted a chair next to his and sagged into it. Powell, editor of the Quimera County *Gazette* was as skinny as Winters was bulky; they were old cronies.

"Can't blame yourself, Ritchie," he offered, reading the sheriff's mind. "Nor the deputy on patrol."

"Had to be the same outfit," opined Winters.

"Same outfit?" asked Powell.

"There's a pattern." Though he never claimed to be a master detective, Winters could add two and two. "This robbery brings others to mind. There's always a distraction, Lorin."

"That's the common denominator, huh?" prodded Powell.

"Think about it," invited Winters. "The big fire in Albuquerque a little while back, a three-storey hotel a fair distance from a bank. Most of the guests got out alive . . ."

"But two burned to death," recalled Powell.

"Fire-fighters, rescue parties trying to help, every lawman on the scene to control the crowds while, three blocks away, the bandits marched into that bank and looted it," said Winters. "Hell, Lorin, you know all the facts, ran a report in your paper."

"The bank manager knifed to death," muttered Powell. "Poor feller must've

5

tried to resist them. And that unfortunate cashier. After he unlocked the safe for them, he must've made a wrong move. Last I heard, an Albuquerque doctor had done everything possible for him, but he'll never be the same. Permanent brain damage. They must've gunwhipped him."

"About a month before the Albuquerque job, there was that daylight bank robbery at Farnum City," Winters reminded him. "Farnum's big day, Congressman Jefford arriving on the early afternoon train to visit his brother, who happened to be mayor of Farnum City. So where was everybody, including the local law, the entire administration and three-quarters of the population?"

"Crowded down by the railroad depot to give the congressman a big welcome," nodded Powell.

"While, uptown, masked gun-toters were taking the Citizens' and Cattlemen's Bank," said Winters. "See what I mean by a pattern? Quite a brain, the hombre bossing that outfit. We got no descriptions, no way of knowing if any of 'em has a record. They're all anonymous. *Has* to be the same outfit. You're right about a common denominator."

"The No Name Gang," mused Powell. "I can't claim credit for cooking up that title for them. A Santa Fe newsman beat me to it."

"It sure fits," Winters said grimly.

The depot of the Hamilton Stage Line was located in clear view, just a short distance from the porch of the sheriff's office. A westbound coach was about to leave, its three spans in harness, the guard securing baggage to the roof, passengers about to board. To divert his friend from his black mood, Powell, a compulsive busybody, began identifying the travellers.

"The stout, important-looking gent is none other than Horace Kolbe if you please. Maybe you haven't heard of Kolbe Enterprises of Los Angeles. He founded it. The company's all caught up in real estate, owns the biggest stores in Los Angeles and three of the best hotels. It seems Mister Kolbe's homebound from visiting a sick relative in Oklahoma."

"He does look important," Winters observed. "Typical big shot."

"Tall feller in black, as if you haven't guessed, is a non-denominational preacher, one of those itinerant sin-killers," offered Powell. "Name of Faber. That's his wife, the colorless woman with the poke bonnet."

"They've been here a couple of weeks I think," said Winters.

"About that long," said Powell. "Last Sunday, Deacon Travis of the Chapel Of Loyal Witness did Mister Faber the courtesy of inviting him to preach the sermon. I'm told Faber preached a doozy — the congregation almost applauded. You know the pudgy jasper in the fancy vest of course."

"Gambler," nodded Winters. "Drifting sporting man, Jerry Arville. He worked all the saloons here. Just another

8

tinhorn. How about the feller in grey?"

"Name of Sanders," said Powell. "Engineer. Destination Vargas, Arizona. Been a silver strike there, new mines opening up. And you know what they say. If a mine's safe, it's because a regular engineer has planned and supervised the drilling of shafts."

"Last, the fiery Brodie girl," muttered Winters, wincing.

"She's being run out of town and the Full Hand Saloon will know her no more," drawled the newspaperman. "Don't take it so hard, Ritchie. There'll always be pressure a sheriff has to submit to."

"Mayor Hapthorne's wife, the old biddy," grouched Winters. "Her and her colleagues of the Ladies Reform League raising hell, calling Chris Brodie a menace to married men, a siren for Pete's sake. The girl's flashy, sure, always giving the customers the glad eye, but I know for a fact she's never encouraged the attentions of family men. And we both know which married man was making a play for her, don't we?"

"Mayor Lucius Hapthorne himself," grinned Powell. "But that'll be our secret, huh? Any mention of the mayor's roving eye in the *Gazette* and *I'd* be run out of town."

"New, aren't they, the crew?" asked Winters. Then he shook his head. "No, I've seen that driver, the guard too, manning Hamilton stages recently."

"Been with the line about six months I'd say," remarked Powell.

★ ★ ★

At the time the westbound stage departed the county seat on schedule, Lawrence Valentine and Woodville Emerson, better known to the law, the lawless and the frontier press as Larry and Stretch, were lazily finishing a fish breakfast in their temporary hideaway far to the southwest.

Rarely did the strife-prone drifters,

10

usually referred to as the Texas Trouble-Shooters, enjoy respite from the rigors and stress of outlaw-fighting. Respite, peace of mind, freedom from tension had been denied them far too long, so it was with profound gratitude that they had relaxed in this out-of-the-way haven, a ghost town called Midas Mound, for the past eight days.

"We bought us plenty of everything in San Raphael," the taller Texan enthused, deftly discarding a fishbone. "Got coffee, booze, tobacco and a whole mess of canned chow and, hereabouts, the huntin's good, so who could ask for anything more?"

Stretch's nickname fitted. He was six and a half feet of sandy-haired Texas beanpole, his gangling frame belying his prodigious muscle-power. Homely as they come, of easy disposition, he had been Larry Valentine's partner most of their lives. Well, they had buddied up as runaway schoolboys, tall for their tender years, at a recruitment centre right after the Civil War began, and that was a long time back. Both had been born and raised in the Texas Panhandle, cattle country. So, like his partner, his natural attire was cowhand's rig. Unlike his partner, he packed a second Colt; with handguns he was ambidextrous.

Larry finished eating and, as he started on his coffee, remarked, "Fishin's good too. Right handy, that creek south a ways. Cut-off from the Rio Bravo I guess."

As dark as his companero was fair, he was of uncommonly brawny build and only three inches shorter. Stretch, and only Stretch, frequently addressed him as 'runt'. Of the two, Larry had the more agile mentality, was the planner, the decision-maker. Altruism was a characteristic he shared with Stretch, and it could have been argued selfishness would be healthier for them.

Were these wanderers dedicated only to their own welfare, selfishly maintaining indifference to the crises afflicting the law-abiding and God-fearing of the frontier, they would have known a great deal more of the peace and quiet they now enjoyed. But they were, as many newsmen had called them, 19th Century knights errant, lacking whatever cussedness it took to turn the blind eye and the deaf ear to the plight of the oppressed and defenseless. Violence was their destiny it seemed. Wherever they travelled, they invariably locked horns with their natural enemies, the lawless, and lawless was a term applicable to all the two-legged predators running foul of town or Federal marshals, county sheriffs, any duly-appointed peace officer. The trouble-shooters had outfought every kind of desperado, stage robbers, rustlers, bank bandits, claim-jumpers, plus a wide cross-section of bunko artists, cardsharps and other swindlers.

In the process, they had earned a reputation they bitterly resented. Many of their victories against the forces of lawlessness had been exaggerated by a hundred and one newspapermen and, to their chagrin, their notoriety had caught up on them far too often.

But now they had peace. For men of their humble needs, could there be a hangout as tranquil as Midas Mound?

"Lucky day for us." This Stretch declared when they had finished their coffee and were building their first cigarettes of the day. "The day we drifted into San Raphael and ran into the feller that told us of this place."

"I knew it'd be the place for us, and it sure is," Larry said contentedly.

One ghost town, they had learned, was not necessarily a replica of every other ghost town. To them, Midas Mound was special in that it had been abandoned only a year ago, and the hardtoiling goldseekers who had quit in disgust had taken a lot, but not everything, with them. There had been only one saloon here. The drifters now squatted in its doorway, catching the morning breeze and staring across to the ugly bulk, the great mound for

14

which the miners had named their camp. One saloon had been enough; the number of shacks left and right of the saloon indicated it had not been a large camp — for the obvious reason that there was no gold to be found here.

Three shaftheads sealed with planks was all that remained to testify to the energetic efforts of the optimists. The mound dominated the area. What buildings there were had been erected in a line opposite it, so the area between had been Midas Mound's only street. Further north was a stoutly-constructed ten-stall livery stable wherein Larry's sorrel and his partner's pinto rested comfortably.

"I wonder what it was called, this saloon," mused Stretch, but not with intense curiosity.

"We'll never know, on account of he took the signboard with him, along with the mirror back of the bar, a lot of furniture and all the booze," grinned Larry. "But that don't matter. What he left behind is what matters."

"Sure enough," agreed Stretch. "Stove in the kitchen that works fine, cutlery and a few cups and plates, lamps, candles and a couple cans of coal-oil he must've forgot."

"They didn't break up all the shacks," drawled Larry. "Some of 'em're passable snug, keep the weather out. We learned that the night of the big storm."

"That was First July, wasn't it?" asked Stretch.

"Might've been," shrugged Larry.

"So maybe today's Fourth of July," suggested Stretch. "Or yesterday was or tomorrow'll be. Well, no matter. A happy Fourth of July to you, Mister Valentine, Suh."

"Same to you, Mister Emerson, Suh," said Larry.

"Do we care we ain't in no crowded town for the holiday?" grinned Stretch.

"We don't care a damn," declared Larry.

"Ain't that the truth," agreed Stretch.

"Would we trade all this peace and quiet for some noisy New Mexico town?" challenged Larry.

"No, we wouldn't." Stretch spoke wistfully. "This place is right for us, runt. A ghost town that ain't had time to crumble. And it's all ours for as long as we want to stay on."

Larry nodded to the still usable well a short distance from the saloon.

"That's as far as we have to fetch good sweet water," he said. "Firewood, plenty of that around. And the creek south where the fish're jumpin', we could walk there 'cept our horses'd get too fat from no exercise."

"I guess your feet ain't itchin'," said Stretch. "You ain't restless, hankerin' to move on."

"Not so you'd notice," Larry assured him.

"So I guess we'll stay put till we've used up our booze and tobacco, huh?" prodded Stretch. "Tell you what, runt. When that happens, we could head for San Raphael, load up more supplies

17

and come right on back here."

"We could do that," nodded Larry. "I don't plan on gettin' weary of Midas Mound."

"And we got plenty dinero, the bankroll's kind of healthy, right?" said Stretch. "Buy everything we need in San Raphael, maybe more booze and tobacco than last time." He glanced casually at his partner's hip pocket. "Just how much . . . ?"

"Plenty, like you said." Larry was custodian of their joint funds, but only because he owned a wallet. "Better'n eight hundred."

"So what d'you say?" asked Stretch.

"Sounds good to me," said Larry. "Got a good thing goin' for us here, livin' lazy, eatin' regular — and no hassles."

"Hassles," reflected Stretch. "Been too many for us, runt."

"One damn ruckus after another," grouched Larry. He dribbled smoke through his nose and grimaced. "And I've had my bellyful of it."

"You and me both," muttered Stretch.

They aired this grievance often. Case-hardened though they were, survivors of countless violent showdowns and with the scars to prove it, they were conscious of their mortality and never fooled themselves. Let journalists go to extremes, describe them as supermen and unbeatable. The trouble-shooters knew better. Whatever their faults, they were realists.

For the present, however, they had found an ideal haven. Midas Mound was all theirs and for an indefinite period, they hoped.

★ ★ ★

The driver and guard of the westbound were keeping their eyes on the trail ahead and the terrain to north and south. The passengers, like travellers the world over, were getting into conversation and proving to be a mixed half-dozen. Pudgy Jerry Arville got the talk started by letting it be known he

19

was headed for Yatesburg, Arizona, to try his luck at the games of chance in a new gambling house there.

"Arville's the name, poker's my game," he grinned. "We'll be nooning at a way station, Piper's Spring, and overnighting in San Raphael. Any of you gents crave a little action, we could maybe get together after supper. I know a good saloon in San Raphael. Carmody's Palace."

"I only gamble on certainties," declared Horace Kolbe Esquire. "I am, sir, an astute businessman, not a speculator. It is only by careful planning and prudent investment of my financial resources that I have built Kolbe Enterprises into the thriving operation it is today, the most progressive in Los Angeles. Gambling is for muddle-headed optimists, I always say."

"Okay, Mister Kolbe," shrugged Arville, transferring his attention to the man in grey. "How about you, friend?"

The garishly-attired Chris Brodie had

been covertly appraising Mr Whitney Sanders, the handsome traveller whose flat-crowned Stetson was the same shade of grey as his well-tailored suit. The only contrasts were his black boots, white shirt and black string necktie. He rejected the gambler's invitation, but with a good-humored grin.

"Thanks just the same. I never got around to mastering the intricacies of poker nor any other games of chance. My work can be demanding, requiring a great deal of concentration."

"What's your line?" Arville was shamelessly inquisitive.

"I'm an engineer," said Sanders.

"Mining?" prodded Arville.

"Some work for the railroads," said Sanders. "But mostly mining projects, new operations such as the Simmons and Cole claim at Vargas, my destination."

"Vargas, that's in Arizona too, right?" said Arville.

"Some forty miles north of Yatesburg I believe," nodded Sanders.

The coach rounded a bend. Arville momentarily slumped against Kolbe, who gave vent to a criticism of the discomforts of travelling by stagecoach.

"Some of you people may be used to it — I'm not," he complained. "I'll be thankful to transfer to a train upon our reaching Pineda Junction in Arizona. The railroad is infinitely preferable, a gentleman's mode of travel."

"Only the best of everything for the rich and powerful, huh Mister Kolbe?" suggested Arville.

The black-garbed, sallow-complexioned Mathew Faber spoke up, his dark eyes gleaming with the fervor of the evangelist.

"What doth it profit a man," he quoted to Kolbe, "that he gain the whole world, but lose his immortal soul?"

"Sir, Reverend, or whatever you call yourself, I do not agree with the theory that wealth is a ticket to damnation," Kolbe curtly retorted.

"I urge you to change your ways,

Brother Arville," Faber pleaded with the sporting gent. "Games of chance bring out the beast in man. Houses providing gambling are houses of sin."

"Amen," his wife said respectfully.

Chris Brodie eyed her askance. What could she, a flashily-garbed redhead, a saloon entertainer, have in common with this demure, butter-wouldn't-melt brunette?

"And you, Sister." Faber's eyes were on her now. "You would, I assure you, find true contentment and be at peace with your Maker, were you to abandon your waywardness and tread the paths of virtue."

The redhead flushed angrily and aired her own grouch.

"Why, I'd like to know, does every sonofagun think he knows all about saloon girls?" she demanded. "It burns me up, the way do-gooders take it for granted a girl's no better'n she ought to be if she works saloons."

"You're right, Chris honey," agreed Arville. "I call it victimization, the way you got run out of Quimera. I was hanging around the Full Hand long enough to know you got a raw deal."

"All the customers get from me is the glad eye, some singin' and a few laughs," she defiantly informed the preacher.

She amused Sanders, but he kept his thoughts to himself. He had already decided she must be color-blind. The fire-red hair, he conceded, was natural, owing nothing to dye, henna for instance. Though he didn't claim to any expert knowledge of female fashion, it was all too obvious to him that this feisty entertainer had much to learn about color co-ordination. On redheads, bright violet and pink just didn't seem right. And, ye gods, the headgear — a straw chapeau festooned with a dazzling confusion of artificial berries and felt flowers every color of the rainbow; it could be said of Miss Christine Brodie that she had visibility plus.

He tactfully remarked, "People do

jump to conclusions, Miss Brodie. Your indignation is justified." Now he changed the subject by aiming a polite question at Faber. "I take it you're on your way to a town in need of a preacher?"

"There'll be such a town somewhere beyond San Raphael," said Faber. "A small place perhaps, inhabited by good folk hungering for spiritual guidance."

Gently, Dora Faber explained, "My dear husband's ministry is any place he's needed."

"Commendable I'm sure," shrugged Kolbe.

Conversation lapsed. Arville tipped his derby over his brow and dozed. Chris brooded. Kolbe disapprovingly surveyed the terrain they now travelled. Not so the Fabers, who apparently thought it beautiful. Sanders was content to stay quiet and give some thought to the work awaiting him at Vargas. Some mining speculators, as he knew from experience, tended to be pinch-penny about safety measures, wanting to cut costs. He hoped Messrs Simmons and Cole were not of that type.

It was almost 11 a.m. by his watch when he became conscious the coach was slowing. His fellow-passengers also noticed. Arville thrust his head out a window to stare ahead.

"The driver is reducing speed," complained Kolbe.

"And I can't see why," said the gambler, withdrawing his head. "High country ahead. We ought to be rolling through Fortuna Pass in a half-hour. This team's gonna be hauling us up a grade, but it's too early for — hey! I think we're stopping."

"Delays, delays," fretted Kolbe.

Driver Caleb Rossiter had reason enough for slowing his team to a halt. A lone rider was approaching from the west, signalling him to do so. Beside him, the scrawny, slack-jawed guard, Groot Mallick, squinted perplexedly.

"What the hell, Caleb?"

"Couldn't be a hold-up," decided

Rossiter, after a quick scan of the immediate vicinity. "Nobody else in sight and no place they could be takin' cover. You better tell the folks inside. Some of 'em might be spooked."

Mallick leaned from his perch to assure the passengers, "It don't look like trouble, so don't nobody fret. Just one rider comin' our way . . . "

"Lawman," observed Rossiter. "I see his badge now."

"A lawman," Mallick informed the travellers. "So you folks breathe easy. Lawmen don't hold up coaches."

"What do you make of this?" Arville asked the engineer.

"We'll find out when the lawman reaches us," shrugged Sanders. "Till then, why he's stopping us is anybody's guess."

"The Lord preserve us!" cried Dora Faber. "He may be coming to warn us of road agents!"

"Now, my dear . . . " began Faber.

"If he's as dumb as some tin stars I've known, he could be lost and

27

wantin' to know where he is," Chris said caustically.

The horseman veered to the left of the standing team to rein up beside the vehicle and address the crew. He was young for a lawman; the gambler pegged him to be twenty-two at most, a fresh-faced, clean-shaven individual whose attire was neat.

"This is about where I figured I'd find you," he told the driver. "Covington's the name, John Covington, deputy sheriff from San Raphael."

"All right, Deputy, what's up?" demanded Rossiter.

"Better you should ask what's down," replied Covington. He doffed his Stetson. All of them curious, some of them craving to stretch their legs, the passengers were climbing out. "Morning, ladies, gents. Sorry about this, but you can blame it on Mother Nature and the big storm a few days back. Fortuna Pass is blocked."

"This is *too* much!" protested Kolbe.

"Avalanche?" asked Sanders.

"Right," nodded the deputy. "We only learned of it early this morning. One of Nick Piper's sons — the family that runs the relay station — he was getting in a little hunting late yesterday and, when he saw what'd happened at the pass, rode back to the Spring to tell his pa. Nick put him on a fresh horse and sent him to San Raphael to spread the word — the boy had to ride all night."

"So, to find us, you had to ride clear around the high country," guessed Sanders.

"Sheriff Lunceford's orders, sir," said Covington. "I was lucky, found a couple short-cuts, but too narrow for a rig and team."

"This pass is the only way through to San Raphael?" frowned Faber.

"For folks travelling by stagecoach, yes," nodded Covington.

"Preposterous state of affairs," scowled Kolbe. "Can't something be done?"

"Oh, dear!" exclaimed Mrs Faber. "Are we to be stranded?"

"Here in this infernal wilderness?" challenged Kolbe.

"How about it, Deputy?" asked Mallick. "Pass gonna be cleared?"

"Well, sure," said Covington. "Everything that can be done'll be done and — uh — it's an emergency so they're getting started on it already. Sheriff organized volunteers. They ought to be at the pass pretty soon, but it's a big pile-up, so they're gonna have to set charges and that's a chore for experts, so there'll be diggers and powder hands on their way from the Sun Flats goldfields."

"Major operation," mused Sanders.

"How long'll it take?" Rossiter asked the deputy.

"No telling for sure," said Covington. "But we figure forty-eight hours is as soon as they could clear a strip wide enough for you to drive the coach through."

"That's unacceptable!" blustered Kolbe. "I have urgent commitments in Los Angeles! It's imperative I reach

Pineda Junction in time to transfer to a westbound train."

"Hey, big shot," growled the redhead, showing her exasperation. "You think you're the only traveller gettin' slowed down? If you're so smart a businessman, you ought to be able to count. There's six of us."

"Young woman, I do not appreciate your impertinence," chided Kolbe.

"What can we do?" wondered Arville. "I mean, we can't wait it out right here."

"What do you say, driver?" asked Sanders. "Must we return to Quimera?"

"Forget it," Chris said flatly. "I *can't* go back. I'm barred from Quimera."

"There's another place you could head for," offered the deputy. "It's not a regular town, but you'd get there faster than it'd take to travel back to Quimera, and there's good shelter and plenty water, feed grass round there for the team too. I could show you the way. You'd make Midas Mound before sundown."

"Midas Mound?" prodded Arville.

"Southwest of here," said Covington. "It used to be a mine camp."

"*Used* to be?" Kolbe turned beetroot-purple.

"For pity's sake, Deputy, are you suggesting we should shelter in a *ghost town*? This is the last straw!"

"Look, what it means is you got a choice, Quimera or Midas Mound," Covington patiently explained. "The Mound's closer and I wouldn't call it a ghost town, not yet anyway. You see, the miners didn't quit till around a year ago, so it's not falling to pieces yet. I know. I took a look at it a couple of weeks back in my own time. The well still works and there are cabins still standing and a creek a little way south. Up to you folks but, if it was me, I'd settle for Midas Mound. It'll likely be my job to come tell you when the pass is cleared, so you'd be on your way again sooner than if you headed back to Quimera." To the crew, he added, "There's even a barn, so your

32

team'd have shelter too."

"And how, may I enquire, would we subsist?" demanded Kolbe.

"Forty-eight hours — without food," groaned Mrs Faber.

"A long period of fasting, Dora," said her husband.

"I notice you got a rifle up there along with the shotgun," Covington observed. "Well, between here and Midas Mound, the hunting's fine. You'd probably score on quail or jackrabbit before you got there. And the creek's good for fishing."

"You got somethin' to say about this, preacher?" Rossiter asked.

"Well . . ." began Faber.

"It seems to me we'll have to wait at Midas Mound," declared Sanders. "But let's discuss it by all means."

2

Roughing It

FINDING himself the centre of attention, the engineer squatted on a flat rock, lit a cigar and made his point, first stressing that his fellow-travellers were entitled to disagree. The question was simple, he suggested. How urgently did the majority of them need to reach their ultimate destinations. Mr Kolbe had made his situation all too clear. He, Sanders, was expected in Vargas, Arizona; the sooner he reached the Simmons and Cole mining site and completed his survey, the sooner the drilling of shafts could begin.

"I'm presuming you left Quimera of your own accord and would as soon not return," he remarked to Arville. "Mister and Mrs Faber must decide as they wish of course — and we all understand Miss Brodie's situation. That's my view of our little predicament. Thanks for listening. Does anybody else have an opinion?"

"For sustenance, we'd be dependent on game shot by the coach crew?" Kolbe asked dubiously.

"Well, the deputy said the hunting's good hereabouts," Arville reminded him.

"Mister, jackrabbit stew mightn't be your idea of fancy chow," said Chris, her eyes on Kolbe, "but it beats stayin' hungry."

"It's for sure you'll down a quail or two," Covington told the guard.

"Mathew?" frowned the preacher's wife.

"We must be unselfish, Dora," he said. "I feel for Brother Kolbe. The pressures of business must weigh heavily upon him, and Brother Sanders's work is of great importance. We have, have we not, heard of terrible tragedies at goldfields, the collapse of tunnels ineptly constructed, unfortunate miners buried alive?"

"You're so right, Mathew," she sighed. "It is our duty to put their needs first."

Young Covington dismounted and hunkered to build a cigarette. During a break in the discussion, he spoke of his recent inspection of the abandoned mine camp, emphasizing again that most of the shacks put up by the prospectors were in fair condition. The biggest building, he told the people, had obviously been the camp's only saloon. It was single-storeyed, but sizeable, and the kitchen out back in good order.

"I remember I downed a quail on my way there," he said. "Didn't have to roast my lunch over a campfire, no siree. Stove in that kitchen works just fine. Feller that ran the saloon, he even left plates and stuff behind, couple tables and some chairs too. You folks'd be comfortable enough waiting there. And don't forget I'd get the good word to you a whole lot faster, soon as

36

the pass is cleared."

"As our driver, what is your opinion?" Kolbe asked Rossiter. "I suppose you could be likened to a ship's captain in a situation of this kind."

"Well, I've been thinkin' on it," frowned Rossiter. "Deputy, me and Groot've worked this run before. We got a lot of high country west of us with Piper's Spring Station on the other side. You sure we can't travel round the mountains, make a wide half-circle maybe?"

"For a stagecoach, it'd take a long time," declared Covington. "There's no other trail, just the stage route through the pass. By horseback a man can ride short-cuts, game tracks and such. By stagecoach, no, it just can't be done."

"My job's to get you folks safe to the way station, then San Raphael and points west," Rossiter told the passengers. "You got a right to vote if we're to turn back to Quimera or hole up at Midas Mound, but . . . "

"I'd try for Midas Mound," said the driver. "If my partner can bring down some fresh meat on our way there — and the deputy claims that's a certainty — it's for sure we'll have food enough. We miss out on lunch at Piper's Spring but, makin' the old camp by sundown, we'll eat hearty I figure. Groot's good with that rifle of his."

"Said you can guide us there," Mallick reminded Covington.

"You won't need a guide," said Covington. "All I got to do is stay with you for about another quarter-mile west. Then you'll see the cut-off to a trail that'll take you clear to the Mound. Rougher trail than the one you're on, but you'll make it. And it'll take you through some mighty pretty country — plenty game for the shooting."

The crew eyed the passengers impatiently. To them, further discussion seemed pointless.

"I guess it has to be Midas Mound,"

shrugged Arville.

"We appear to have no choice," grouched Kolbe. "But I won't enjoy this experience."

"So," said Rossiter. "Everybody back on board and we'll get goin' again."

Climbing up to take his position beside the driver, Mallick discarded his shotgun in favour of his Winchester. He was readying that weapon when Covington remounted and the passengers reboarded.

After leading the coach another quarter-mile west, the deputy indicated the cut-off to the Midas Mound trail and, as Rossiter turned his team, repeated his promise; he would make for the Mound with all speed as soon as the pass was cleared.

For the passengers, the going was bumpier now. They were jolted and there were frequent pauses. Mallick's Winchester barked, and he was scoring.

"I guess it could take longer than forty-eight hours," Arville remarked, much to Kolbe's chagrin. "The deputy could only give us a rough idea, huh?"

His question was directed at Sanders.

"Hard for me to say," shrugged the engineer. "Without seeing the pile-up I mean. And this is strange territory to me, I've never travelled through Fortuna Pass. Have any of you?"

"Me, a few years back," offered Arville.

"What can you remember of it?" asked Sanders. "Is it a wide passage through the mountains, or narrow?"

"Narrow as I recall," frowned Arville. "Wouldn't be more than thirty yards wide. And, oh yeah, the rockwalls both sides of the trail're steep and real high."

"The crew from the goldfields, and especially the explosives experts, will have to work carefully," Sanders declared. "They daren't rush this chore."

"All very encouraging — I don't think," grimaced Kolbe.

"Sorry," said Sanders. "No point in my understating what I believe to be a dangerous project. The conditions, you see — a narrow pass and highwalled. There'll have to be a quantity of rock and rubble cleared manually before charges can be set, and that'll be a delicate operation. Vibration, Mister Kolbe, the danger of a second avalanche."

"How can these terrible things happen?" murmured Mrs Faber.

"The recent storm would be the culprit, in my opinion," said Sanders. "Prolonged rain — heavy rain — loosens earth, and not just at ground level. At high points, such as the heights above the pass, the downpour could've started earth shifting, also shale, any kind of rubble between and under rocks. That's all it takes, Mrs Faber. If one high rock comes free, falls, dislodging other rocks . . . " He spread his hands, "you have an avalanche."

Again, the coach lurched to a halt. The guard's rifle barked. Sanders glanced to a window and quickly changed position, drawing a pistol

41

from under his coat and muttering an apology for having to lean past Chris. From the window, his handgun, a Smith & Wesson .38 with shortened barrel, added the din of two reports to the clamor of Mallick's Winchester. He returned to his seat, restoring the .38 to its armpit holster and flashing a reassuring grin. They heard Mallick drop from his perch to go collect kills.

"Do any good?" asked the gambler.

"Missed with my first shot, brought one bird down with my second," said Sanders. "I'm no sharpshooter, but the guard's doing well for us. We'll not starve at Midas Mound."

"Madam, you are a skilled cook, dare I hope?" Kolbe asked Mrs Faber.

"I do my best, sir," she said demurely.

Never demure, Chris aimed a less than amiable glance in Kolbe's direction.

"You didn't think to ask *me*, but I'll tell you anyway," she said. "I can gut and scale fish, pluck and cook chicken, quail, turkey, any kind of bird, and dish it up like it'd melt in your mouth. So don't fret, big shot. You'll eat good tonight."

"Must you be so aggressive, young woman?" chided Kolbe.

"You got a temper same color as your hair," commented Arville.

"I got feelin's like anybody else," Chris retorted. "It riles me when high-toned folks look at me like I'm dirt. I don't take kindly to that. Why the hell should I?"

"Language, Sister!" gasped Faber.

"Aw, forget it," scowled Chris.

"Look, folks, we're gonna have to get along," cajoled the gambler. "We're all in the same boat. Well, the same coach. Stuck with one another till the pass is clear and we make San Raphael, right? It's gonna get plenty unsociable unless we stay friendly. Anyway, we can try, can't we?"

Kolbe fixed a challenging eye on the engineer. The coach was rolling again. And none too smoothly, adding discomfort to his displeasure.

"Sir, you find our predicament amusing?"

Sanders erased his grin and insisted, "It has its humorous side. When a mixed half-dozen, six travellers of varying backgrounds, get thrown together this way, and with the prospect of staying together for some little time, there are personality clashes. It's inevitable, I guess."

"And you think that's funny?" demanded Chris.

"To some degree, yes, Miss Brodie," he nodded.

"I guess it'd be some kind of miracle," reflected Arville. "Six passengers in a coach, they couldn't be all exactly the same. Like for instance six preachers, six engineers, six sporting men . . . "

"I commend you for your appeal of a few moments ago, Brother," Faber said warmly. "We differ in many ways but, as Christians, we should endeavor to endure our situation and avoid ill will toward one another. Patience, my friends. We should be patient, controlling our emotions."

"Amen," said his wife.

"Men of the cloth can afford patience," retorted Kolbe. "For business men — burdened by heavy responsibilities — patience is not always possible."

"I suppose," suggested Sanders, "We'll just have to make the best of a difficult situation."

"I will try," promised Mrs Faber. "Yes, I must put my faith in the Lord and strive to forget my fears."

"We got nothing to be afraid of anyway," opined Arville.

"Ghost town is perhaps an unfortunate way of describing a deserted mining town, my dear," soothed Faber.

"It's just an expression," shrugged Sanders. "And we're lucky. According to Deputy Covington, Midas Mound was abandoned only twelve months ago. How much deterioration can occur in just one year? So, it seems to me we could be far worse off."

"Sleeping arrangements will be primitive," Kolbe sombrely predicted.

"When you're weary enough, you sleep, no matter what," retorted Chris.

"Let's all look on the bright side, huh?" urged Arville. "Deputy said there's shacks still weatherproof. We'll have the whole place to ourselves, so there'll be space for everybody. Even for the team, he said."

"Travellers have had to rough it in far worse conditions," said Sanders.

"Does it have to take all afternoon for us to get there?" grouched the redhead. "I ate scarce any breakfast this mornin' and now my stomach thinks my throat's cut."

"That's a disgusting expression," sniffed Kolbe.

"Do me a favor, sportin' man," Chris begged the gambler. "If I stick my head out a window, I'll lose the only hat I got. How about *you* stick your head out and ask the driver why can't this rig roll faster?"

"Probably impossible, Sister," protested

Faber. "This is a rough trail."

"No harm in asking," shrugged Arville. He removed his derby, poked his head out a window and called the question. "Hey, driver! This as fast as we can go?"

They listened to Rossiter's bellowed reply.

"We got plenty fresh meat! Trail ahead's lookin' clearer, so I'll try hustlin' this team in a little while — but everybody hang on!"

Arville resumed his seat, grinning cheerfully.

"We could do it — get there before dark," he suggested.

The driver urged his three spans to greater speed a short time later and, as the afternoon wore on, the passengers' discomfort increased. The Fabers clung to each other. Chris loosed an unladylike remark or two each time her garish headgear came askew. Kolbe glared when the gambler slumped against him.

Not until 4.15 or thereabouts did

Rossiter ease the pace.

"*Now* why are we slowing down?" demanded the exasperated Kolbe.

Sanders doffed his hat, begged the redhead's pardon and leaned across her to thrust his head out and stare forward past the plodding team. All eyes were on him when he resumed his seat.

"I'd say our driver's just being cautious," he told his companions.

"You see anything ahead?" demanded Chris.

"Smoke," said Sanders.

"Oh, no!" gasped Mrs Faber. "Not a brush fire, please God!"

"Be calm, Dora," said her husband.

"Definitely not a brush fire," said Sanders. "Just enough of it to be visible at this distance. More like campfire smoke or, if we're getting close to our destination, smoke from a chimney."

"Indicating somebody else could be in occupation?" frowned Kolbe.

"For our sake, it better not be a bunch of outlaws holed up," mumbled Arville.

"Let us not fear the worst, my friend," pleaded Faber.

"The driver's just being cautious," Sanders repeated. "A natural reaction. We should be grateful our crew is so observant. And well-armed, come to think of it. Sidearms, as well as the shotgun and Winchester." He nodded encouragingly to Mrs Faber. "No need to assume there'll be trouble. Whoever else is sheltering at Midas Mound will probably be harmless, posing no threat to our welfare."

Up top, Mallick was cocking his shotgun. In their slow approach to the mound and the line of adobe and plank buildings facing it, he and Rossiter were using their eyes.

"What d'you make of it?" he muttered.

"Nobody turnin' out to look our way," observed Rossiter. "Couple more minutes and they'll hear us. Then we'll see how many."

The Texans had not yet lost their appetite for fish. They were in the saloon kitchen, Larry was dropping fresh grinds into the filled coffee pot, Stretch setting the skillet in position, when they heard the sounds that could only mean one thing — adios privacy, peace and quiet, seclusion.

The taller drifter was at once fatalistic and pleading for reason.

"We're lucky it didn't happen before now, runt. Must be hundreds of folks know this place, know there's water here."

"No use complainin'," Larry agreed. "But we'd better look 'em over rightaway. First thing we need to know is are they friendlies or hostiles."

They were bareheaded, but strapping on their Colts when they quit the kitchen, crossed the barroom and stepped out into the waning sunlight.

"Stagecoach." Stretch was taken aback. "Holy Hannah, *this* ain't no stage stop."

"Like I always say . . . " began Larry.

"Yup," nodded Stretch. "Got to be a reason for everything."

50

As the coach rolled to a halt, the tall men took note of the guard's shotgun and the fact that the driver's right hand had dropped to the butt of his holstered revolver.

"You got a right to be careful," Larry conceded, his deep baritone carrying clear to crew and passengers. "But, now that you see us, I'd take it kindly if you uncock that scattergun."

"How many of you?" challenged Rossiter.

"You're lookin' at the only other hombres holed up here," drawled Stretch.

"Holed up, huh?" prodded Mallick. "Meanin' hidin' from the law?"

"Not so you'd notice, feller." Larry narrowed his eyes. "My partner and me got nothin' to fear from the law and you travellers got nothin' to fear from us. So, from here on, let's keep it friendly. Put up your weapons and answer *me* a question. What's a stagecoach doin' in a place like this?"

The Texans were offered an explanation by the first passenger to alight, Jerry Arville. The gambler was followed by the Fabers, then by Kolbe. Mallick uncocked his shotgun and shrugged. Next to climb out, Sanders offered his arm and helped the redhead from the vehicle. The preacher added his voice to Arville's report of the blocking of Fortuna Pass after which Kolbe assertively identified himself and insisted the tall men do likewise. This seemed reasonable to Stretch, who treated the travellers to an amiable grin and introduced himself and partner.

"Woodville's my handle. This here's my partner Lawrence."

Not for the first time, the trouble-shooters chose to offer only their given names to strangers. And, as on other such occasions, they nursed the hope none of these people would remember them from old newspaper photographs.

"The crew . . . " began Arville.

"Rossiter and Mallick," growled the driver.

"Right," nodded Arville. "Reverend and Mrs Faber and Miss Brodie. I'm Jerry Arville and this gent's Mister Sanders and — uh — Mister Kolbe already named himself."

"So," said Larry. "Seems like you folks're gonna be stuck here for as long as it takes them toilers to clear the pass."

"We have no option," said Kolbe.

"It never got to be real big, did it?" remarked Chris, gazing about. "Just three tunnels in the mound, some shacks and only one joy-house."

"But shelter enough for all," observed Sanders.

"Uh huh, plenty room," nodded Larry. He glanced to the coach roof. "Huntin' was good 'tween the stage trail and here, huh? Well, we ain't short on chow either, so nobody sleeps hungry tonight." To Rossiter he remarked, "Our horses won't mind company. Plenty stalls for the team in the barn. Want a little help unloadin' the baggage? Your passengers can

53

choose their quarters while there's still daylight . . . "

"And then there'd better be some extra cookin'," suggested Stretch. "We got coffee boilin' and a skillet of fish and that leaves plenty room on the stove for whatever grub the ladies want to cook. Oven's empty too."

"Soon as I find a roof and four walls for restin' my butt, I'll get to pluckin'," Chris promptly announced. "I crave roasted quail, and there'll be enough to go round if anybody else craves some of the same."

The Texans helped unload and distribute baggage, after which Rossiter wheeled his team and made for the livery stable, Mallick glancing backward at fire-haired Chris, toting a battered valise and beelining for a shack. Kolbe and Arville followed her example as did the Fabers. Sanders picked up his grip, moved past the tall men and into the saloon and was studying the bar-room when they joined him.

"I don't snore," he assured them.

"Already guessed this is your sleeping place, but all I need is a corner. So . . . ?"

"Stow your grip and welcome," shrugged Larry.

"I'm obliged," said Sanders. "Been here long?" Stretch told him how long. "So you were roosting here the night of the big storm. Any damage?"

"Old place weathered the storm pretty good," offered Stretch.

"Roof didn't leak?" asked Sanders, raising his eyes.

"We didn't take no water," said Larry. "When the storm quit, we checked the barn and all the shacks. Couple took water, but most of 'em were dry."

"So let's hope my fellow-travellers appreciate their good fortune," said Sanders, setting his grip down. "I think some of them will, but you know how it goes. You can't satisfy everybody."

"If I had to make a guess, I'd peg Mister High and Mighty Kolbe for the big bellyacher," said Stretch.

"Good guess, Woodville," grinned Sanders. "And the preacher's wife is too nervous for her own good."

"But not the strawberry roan filly," guessed Larry.

"Not Chris Brodie." The engineer's grin broadened. "No weakling, that one. Every amorous miner or fired-up ranch-hand who ever took liberties with her, I'm sure they must've regretted it."

Turning to his partner, Larry suggested, "While you're tendin' our supper, I'll tidy up in here, set up what tables and chairs there are."

"Well, sure," nodded Stretch. "We might's well all chow down together."

Sanders chose a corner and was removing a few necessities from his grip, Larry dusting off furniture, when Chris marched in bareheaded, sleeves rolled up and toting four quail.

"Which way to the kitchen?" she demanded.

"Follow your purty nose, Red," directed Larry.

"Much obliged, Big Boy," she said.

And, for the first time, Sanders saw her smile. Great smile, he reflected.

For some time thereafter, Stretch found himself giving thanks the kitchen was spacious. It needed to be, what with the redhead roasting quail and Dora Faber fixing jackrabbit stew.

When it came time for the trouble-shooters to dine on fried fish, the travellers on quail or jackrabbit, Chris, the Fabers and Kolbe claimed chairs and sat at table. The other men squatted cross-legged to satisfy their appetites and, for a while, there was little talk, all the travellers eating hungrily.

Only Chris, the Fabers and the engineer thought to thank the Texans for sharing their coffee supply. The Texans replied they were welcome and decided against mentioning they were as well supplied with rye whiskey; hospitality had to have its limits. Nearing the end of their meal, the Fabers indicated they were well satisfied with the cabin they would share. The only others doubling up were the driver and guard.

By the time they had finished their coffee and the men preparing to smoke, Kolbe was in good voice again, conceding this austere accommodation would suffice for a short stay, but bitterly complaining of the circumstances delaying his return to Los Angeles.

"Circumstances beyond the control of mere mortals, Brother Kolbe," Faber gravely reminded him. "An act of God. And, what God inflicts, man must endure."

Arville offered the preacher a cigar.

"Just a Long Nine," he remarked. "Not as fine as Mister Kolbe's Havanas, but a good enough smoke."

Faber eyed him reproachfully.

"Brother Arville, I have never used tobacco in any form nor alcohol!"

"Never!" said Mrs Faber.

"No offense," shrugged Arville.

"With your permission, ladies?" asked Sanders, producing a cigar.

The preacher's wife winced disdainfully. Not so the redhead, who leaned back in her chair, crossed her legs and said,

"Go ahead, boys. I'm no killjoy."

While the Texans dug out Durhamsacks and began building quirleys, they were surveyed intently by Kolbe. He began questioning them. They didn't much appreciate his curiosity nor his manner of asking questions; it began to sound like an interrogation, but they chose to conceal their resentment.

"You are, of course, out of work cowhands?" he began.

"Easy guess," commented Rossiter. "What else could they be? You see one cattleman, you've seen 'em all."

"Cowhands, sure, but it ain't that we're out of work," Larry told the Los Angeles man.

"What do you mean by that?" persisted Kolbe.

"Hey, Big Shot," chided Chris. "You sure ask a lot of questions."

"I would remind you, Miss Brodie,

that we know nothing of these men," Kolbe said sternly. "If we are to be confined in this desolate place for an indefinite period, it seems to me we've a right to assure ourselves Lawrence and Woodville are trustworthy. For all we know, they could be desperadoes."

"You got a point, mister," frowned Mallick.

"Brother Kolbe, this is most improper," protested Faber. "We are their guests. They have taken us in and . . ."

"You got that wrong, preacher," drawled Larry. "Nobody owns Midas Mound. We found it before you folks, but that don't give us no claim to it."

"What it gets down to is you got as much right to roost here as my buddy and me," explained Stretch.

"Lawrence, you've not yet answered my question," said Kolbe.

"You'll have to ask it again," Larry said, lighting his cigarette. "I plumb forgot it."

"You are cattlemen and obviously at a loose end, yet you claim you aren't out of work?" demanded Kolbe.

"Right," nodded Larry. "We ain't ridin' for no rancher right now. We only work when we got to, meanin' when we run out of cash. Just happens we got cash enough to get by on, savvy?"

"Just enough to get by on," offered Stretch. "So we're restin' easy here, just enjoyin' bein' lazy."

"Doing *nothing*?" challenged Kolbe. "Is that any way for a grown man to live?"

"Up to them, wouldn't you say?" countered Chris. "It's their life."

"I'd be interested to know how long it's been since you held steady jobs," said Kolbe, ignoring her interjection.

"Can you recollect how long?" Larry asked his partner.

"Nope," shrugged Stretch.

"Ah, ha!" Kolbe's eyes gleamed. "If you cannot remember your last regular employment, how could you still be solvent?"

Both Texans frowned perplexedly.

61

Sanders blew a perfect smoke-ring, watched it waft ceilingward and defined the word for them.

"Solvent. Able to settle all debts. Actually, your own definition is self-explanatory. You have sufficient cash for your needs. I think Mister Kolbe's wondering how you can be at leisure and solvent at the same time."

"I await your explanation, Lawrence," Kolbe said grimly.

"Wait no longer," drawled Larry. "Ever hear of poker?"

"Roulette — dice?" prodded Stretch.

"Blackjack, three card monte, faro?" asked Larry. Much to Sanders' amusement, he addressed Mrs Faber contritely. "You won't approve, ma'am but we're confessin' anyway. We gamble a lot. Sometimes we ride a winnin' streak, sometimes Lady Luck vamooses plumb out of sight."

"But, mostly, we break even," said Stretch. "Meanin' we got enough dinero . . . "

"To get by on," smiled Sanders.

"You took the words right out of my mouth," nodded Stretch.

Kolbe shook his head in disgust.

"An uncertain existence, a feckless way of life," he accused. "Have you no ambition?"

"Sure have," declared Larry. "Just one ambition. To mind our own business."

"But man cannot live for himself alone," Faber said earnestly. "The Lord requires that we should have concern for the welfare of our fellow-men."

"Well, we do that," Stretch assured him. "Yup. We like helpin' folks, do it all the time."

"Then there is yet hope for you," said Faber.

Arville spoke up eagerly.

"Gambling men, huh. How about a little action, boys? I just happen to have a new deck. What would you say to a couple hours of five card stud, help kill time?"

"Muchas gracias, but I reckon not," said Larry. "Ain't in the mood, friend.

63

Some other time maybe."

"It's gonna get dull for us here," sighed Arville. "Just waiting it out."

"Patience is a virtue," Mrs Faber instructed him.

"We're lucky to have found good shelter," said Sanders. "Let's be thankful for that much. For as long as we're here, I'm sure we can get along without entertainment. We could all use some rest anyway. It's been quite a day for us, one way or another."

"Rough run from the stage trail to here?" asked Larry.

"Real bone-shaker," winced Arville. He nodded to the crew. "But you fellers did your best by us. We sure appreciate it."

"That's what we're paid for," shrugged Rossiter.

"Sure is quiet," Chris said boredly. "So now I know how a ghost town feels."

"We've bunked in many a ghost town," Larry told her. "Only noise you're liable to hear is a loose plank

64

flappin' in the wind."

"No ghosts?" she grinned. "You ain't seen no spooks?"

"Only two markers we found," said Larry. "That's all the cemetery there is. The grave markers show the names of a couple old prospectors that cashed in about a year and a half ago. Too old for the heavy chores I guess."

"So now they are at peace," muttered Faber.

"Well, they're still in the ground," drawled Stretch. "Ain't been no ghosts pesterin' us."

There was desultory conversation for a while, after which the travellers and crew decided they should call it a day. Soon, only Sanders and the Texans remained in the bar-room; now he could voice a request.

3

By Whose Hand?

"I WAS reluctant to ask before," said the engineer. "The Fabers are typical bluenoses, as you must've noticed. I can imagine the good lady flinching in horror and her man praying for my salvation or, worse still, delivering a sermon."

"They ain't what I'd call joyful folks," nodded Stretch.

"Somethin' you wanted to ask?" prodded Larry.

"Don't misunderstand," said Sanders. "It's not an addiction. I'm a moderate drinker in fact. But, right now, if you can oblige, I'd really appreciate a nightcap — just the one."

"Good timin', Mister Sanders," approved Stretch.

"Let's dispense with the Mister,"

suggested Sanders.

"Just happens we ain't temperance neither," Larry informed him.

"Provisioned up in San Raphael before we came lookin' for Midas Mound," said Stretch. "And, friend, when we provision up, we don't forget nothin' important, like a few bottles of good rye for instance."

"You gonna play barkeep?" asked Larry.

"My pleasure," said Stretch.

Larry found three glasses. From their stashed gear in a corner of the kitchen, Stretch fetched a bottle. He pulled the cork and poured.

"Just the one for us too," Larry told him.

"Sure," nodded Stretch.

He took the bottle away and, when he returned, they took seats at a table. Sanders raised his glass.

"A toast," he suggested.

"Go ahead," invited Larry.

"May the luck stay with you," intoned Sanders. "May fire-haired Miss

Brodie find happiness somewhere, may Mathew Faber be granted many years of fruitful ministry, may Jerry Arville be dealt a pat hand, may Horace Kolbe continue to prosper — as wealth and power seem so damned important to him — and may our driver and guard never encounter hold-up artists."

"I reckon you've covered everything," remarked Larry.

"Bottoms up," said Stretch.

They savored their whiskey. Sanders smacked his lips and commended them on their good taste.

"Excellent rye."

"Sure," agreed Larry. "Well, who needs rotgut?"

"Ain't that the truth," said Stretch.

"You forgot yourself, Sanders," said Larry. "Wished the best of everything for the rest of us, but how about you?"

Sanders downed another mouthful and shrugged.

"All I wish for myself is, when I reach the Simmons and Cole claim out of Vargas, no impatient amateurs

68

have tried boring a shaft," he confided. "Independents, parties of prospectors like those who worked this place, sometimes observe all necessary precautions. Just as many don't. A cave-in is a hell of a thing."

"No argument," Stretch said fervently.

"Drilling operations require careful planning," said Sanders. "And that's an engineer's responsibility. I won't bend your ears with technicalities, but take it from me. Whoever said every man to his job knew what he was talking about."

"If everything's set up right — by a specialist — the shaft's safe," said Larry.

"Yes, my specialty," nodded Sanders. "Well, one of them. To each his own, right? If we three were riding some cattleman's range and sighted a few steers trapped in a tangle of brush, you'd be in your element. You'd know how to free them, but I'd be no help at all."

"That's how it goes," said Larry.

69

When their glasses were empty, they talked for some twenty more minutes before turning in.

The night *seemed* to pass without incident.

As was their wont, the Texans were up early, in the kitchen, stoking up the stove to prepare breakfast for ten. Larry thought to leave his partner long enough to move through the bar-room where the engineer still slept and, from the front doorway, glance along what the builders of this camp had called the street.

So far, only one traveller astir, the tough redhead, now emerging from the shack she had claimed, bareheaded and with soap in hand and a towel and change of underwear over an arm. She paused upon reaching the saloon; he nodded genially.

"Sleep well, Red?"

"Well enough, Tex," she nodded. "The creek's south? I don't eat till I'm clean all over and rid of yesterday's dust."

"Just keep headed south through the brush," he directed. "Swing left when you make the bank and mosey upstream a ways. Shallow up there, good for takin' a bath."

"I'll help dish up breakfast when I get back," she said, moving on.

One by one, the others were appearing when Larry turned back into the saloon, making for the well to draw water for their ablutions. Sanders rose as Larry made for the kitchen, traded nods with him and broke out his shaving gear.

By the time squeaky-clean Chris came bustling in, the drifters were ladling food onto plates and her fellow-passengers trading remarks. She frowned at Mrs Faber, who said defensively,

"I offered to help, but they said 'Just relax, ma'am, we can manage.' Otherwise, I'd have . . ."

"Okay," shrugged Chris. "If they don't need you, they don't need me."

Sanders had claimed a chair this morning, but now caught her eye and

71

rose to hold its back.

"Allow me, Miss Brodie."

"Ain't you the gentleman," she remarked, as he helped seat her.

"Always," he cheerfully assured her. The Texans came in from the kitchen, each toting laden plates. They set them down, returned to the kitchen and repeated this routine until ten breakfasts were served. It was then that the redhead noted,

"We ain't all here."

"Sure we are," said Mallick.

"No," said Sanders. "One absentee, our poker-loving friend Arville."

"He sleeps late," shrugged Kolbe.

"I'll go roust him," offered Stretch.

"No, let me," said Sanders, getting to his feet. "It's more than enough you and Lawrence fixed breakfast for us, and you must be as hungry as we are. I'll go wake him."

He strolled out and breakfast began, the Texans and the redhead setting to with gusto, Mrs Faber and husband less so, Kolbe sniffing each forkful before transferring it to his interior, Rossiter and Mallick wolfing their share.

"Gonna be another hot day," Stretch remarked.

"For sure," nodded Larry. "No chance their chow'll get cold, Sanders and the sportin' gent."

A short time later, Kolbe remarked, "The man must be a heavy sleeper, if Sanders is still trying to wake him."

"If the tinhorn ain't hungry, I'll eat his share," said Rossiter.

The sound of footsteps, slow and measured, heralded the engineer's return. He appeared in the doorway, his clean-cut face devoid of expression. The people eyed him curiously.

"I'm sorry," he said. "There's no easy way of breaking bad news, so I must say it bluntly. I found Jerry Arville dead." Chris's eyebrows shot up. The Texans traded frowns, as did Rossiter and Mallick. Kolbe blinked incredulously. Mrs Faber made a whimpering sound; her husband promptly slid an arm about her shoulders. "It would be better if the ladies remain here."

Larry and Stretch were first on their feet and advancing on Sanders, who moved out into the morning sunlight. They were followed by the stage crew and Kolbe, then Faber. Along to one of the shacks he led them.

"You didn't . . . ?" began Larry.

"No," said Sanders. "I haven't touched anything, didn't as much as grasp his shoulder. When you see him, you'll understand. It was painfully obvious to me he'd never sit down to another breakfast."

"The poor soul, our brother Arville, was stricken, a heart attack perhaps," assumed Faber.

"Gentlemen, death was not from natural causes," declared Sanders, as they reached the shack's doorway. "Arville was murdered."

"*Murdered* . . . ?" gasped Kolbe. "Thunderation!"

"What makes you think . . . ?" began Rossiter.

"You'll see for yourself," said Sanders.

74

He entered the shack with the tall men, the others hovering about the doorway, peering in. It was an ugly scene, the dead man just lying there, a blanket drawn up to his chin, the part covering his chest showing a dry bloodstain and an incision. He had removed only his boots, coat, fancy vest and neckwear before retiring. The boots were beside his valise, the garments hanging from a nail in the rear wall.

"He was an easy mark," muttered Larry. "Somebody just snuck in and stabbed him, and once was enough." He nudged his partner. "You know what to do."

"On my way," said Stretch, and he made his exit, shouldering past the men in the doorway.

"The blood looks — quite dry," observed Sanders, grimacing. "No guessing how many hours ago it happened."

"And chances are he was sleepin' deep," decided Larry.

"Had to be, damn it, else he'd have

hollered and we'd have heard him."

"What's your buddy lookin' for?" demanded Mallick.

He winced impatiently as Faber moved in, dropped to his knees beside the body, bowed his head and clasped his hands in prayer. The guard repeated his question. Larry rose and replied,

"He's scoutin' around. If he cuts sign of a horse, meanin' neither of ours nor a team animal, it'll mean some bastard snuck in late and did this."

"And — if he doesn't?" demanded Kolbe.

"Figure it out for yourself," invited Larry.

The color drained from Kolbe's plump face.

"Surely," he breathed, "you can't mean . . . ?"

"What the hell else can it mean?" challenged Larry. "The tinhorn got his from somebody already here."

"Hold on now . . . " began Rossiter.

"I don't like it any more'n you do," Larry assured him. "But we're gonna have to face up to it. Nothin' else makes sense."

"What should we do next?" wondered Sanders.

"We cover his face, get on back to the saloon and do our palaverin' while we're eatin'," growled Larry. "Maybe some of you lost your appetite. I can understand that. But look at it this way. We can't help this poor sonofagun by stayin' hungry. And, speakin' for myself, I think clearer when my belly's full."

Sanders drew up the blanket to cover the ashen face of the dead man. The taller Texan approached after they quit the shack. His report of his scouting expedition wasn't verbal; he merely shook his head.

Back in the saloon, Sanders shrugged uncomfortably but began eating, as did the Texans and the crew, while the women stared and Kolbe picked at his food, his hands trembling. Mrs Faber's reaction to her husband's informing her the gambler had been murdered irritated the redhead. She moaned and clasped hand to brow, while Chris gave vent to shock and exasperation, rising so quickly that her chair overturned.

"This is plain loco!" she complained. "Who'd want to knife a no-account like him? He was just another gamblin' man and, all the time he was workin' Quimera, he was never in no trouble. No sport ever called him a sharper."

"There'll be discussion, Miss Brodie," Sanders said gently.

"Right," nodded Rossiter. "We got to talk this out, and weepin' and wailin' ain't gonna help none."

"You'll hear no wailin' from *me*," declared Chris. "Preacher, is that wife of yours *ever* gonna quiet down?" She turned away. "The hell with it. I'll fetch the coffee."

Larry set her chair back into position after she disappeared into the kitchen. She returned moments later toting two coffee pots and proceeded to fill cups. Sanders held her chair when she was ready to reseat herself. Then he finished eating and not until everybody had downed as much coffee as they needed was the tense silence broken, predictably by Kolbe.

"I will not *permit* anybody to consider me a suspect!" he blustered.

"Simmer down, mister," Larry chided as he fished out his makings. "Ain't none of us enjoyin' this."

"Woodville could find no strange horse tracks," muttered Sanders.

"And the wind last night wasn't strong enough to sweep out no tracks," said Stretch. "You can look at the ground out front and still see your bootmarks from when you climbed off of the stage yesterday."

"This is — unthinkable!" protested Faber.

"I will not tolerate . . . !" began Kolbe.

"Mister Kolbe, we are all suspects," declared Sanders. "It's that simple."

"And goin' off half-cocked won't get us anywhere," warned Larry. "Sanders told it true. It could've been any of us. No moon last night. Dark out there. Any time after we all turned in, one of us could've gone to that shack, put his knife in Arville, then snuck back to his sleepin' place with nobody seein' or hearin' him. That's how it *had* to be."

"So no use wranglin' about it," Stretch pointed out. He scratched a match, held it to his partner's cigarette, lit his own and suggested, "Better we parley reasonable, no hombre turnin' ornery."

"I got a question," frowned Chris. "Why *didn't* anybody hear anything."

"He was knifed in his sleep, Red," Larry told her. "Just didn't have time to yell. So what could anybody hear?"

"Dumb question," she chided herself.

"Not at all," said Sanders.

"You got a right to ask," nodded Larry. "Any question comes to mind. You or anybody else." He switched his gaze to the driver. "Rossiter, if anybody's in charge here, it's you. So . . . ?"

80

Rossiter scratched at his jowls and squinted uneasily.

"Had to be one of us did it? I don't know. My chore is drivin' coaches, not solvin' riddles."

"You're in command," Sanders pointed out.

"Isn't it obvious the law authorities should be advised, and as quickly as possible?" challenged Kolbe, eyeing the Texans impatiently. "You have saddle animals. One of you should leave at once to report the matter to the Quimera sheriff or, if you can find the deputy's route, to San Raphael."

"Think so, do you?" muttered Mallick. "What if he just keeps ridin'? He could be the killer — gettin' away."

The drifters stifled their natural reaction to Mallick's words; this was no time for a show of temper.

"I think my partner and me agree the guard's makin' sense," Larry said evenly. "We know we didn't kill Arville, but nobody else does. So neither of us — nor anybody else — is ridin' out

81

of here. How does that set with you, Rossiter? Like Sanders, said, you're in command."

"I was never in this kind of situation before," shrugged Rossiter. "So — uh — better somebody else comes up with — well — a notion, a suggestion, *somethin'*."

"We are five travellers, a coach crew and, as they describe themselves, a couple of drifters," said Kolbe. "None of us qualified to conduct a murder investigation."

"Seems we have no choice, Mister Kolbe," said Sanders. "One of us is undoubtedly a murderer. We have to accept that."

Mrs Faber loosed a cry of fear. Her husband comforted her as best he could and appealed to the men.

"You should choose your words with care, brothers, out of deference to the ladies."

"We're all sorry for the ladies," drawled Stretch. "But there's no gettin' round it, is there? We got a killer

82

here, so we got to talk about that and somebody better come up with a notion."

"Anybody got any?" prodded Mallick, glancing around.

"Who would commit such a terrible crime?" wondered Faber.

"Somebody with a reason," said Larry.

"But he was a stranger to us all," argued the preacher. "That is — all but this young lady."

"Are you sayin' . . . ?" flared Chris.

"Take it easy, Red," soothed Larry. "You're one party I'd never point at. But you're the only one knew him."

"Just casual," she frowned. "He was in and out of the Full Hand. All I knew was his name, and we said hallo once in a while."

"Too bad you didn't get to know him close," complained Larry.

"Why?" she demanded.

"Well," said Larry. "If he had a run-in with some hombre in Quimera,

I mean real bad trouble, and if it happened where you were workin', you might remember who it was."

"A grudge-toter," suggested Stretch. "Some jasper that got to hate his gizzard — bad enough to want him dead."

"Can't help you," she shrugged. "He didn't seem the kind to make enemies, just a harmless sport."

"There has to be a motive," insisted Sanders. "One of us had a motive for . . ."

"*Was* there a motive?" countered Kolbe.

"Had to be," declared Larry. "Nobody kills for no reason."

Kolbe's retort started a few scalps crawling.

"A homicidal maniac does. Any of you — I exclude myself of course — any of you could have homicidal tendencies, fixations."

"Now just a doggone minute . . ." began Stretch.

"Such cases aren't unknown," Kolbe

84

said grimly. "Seemingly respectable people who, when afflicted, cannot restrain their urge to kill. And, when it's done, they cunningly revert to the demeanor of the normal person familiar to their friends and neighbours."

"This is causing my wife great distress, Brother Kolbe," chided Faber.

"Hey, remember me?" challenged the redhead. "I'm female too, and I ain't enjoyin' this any more'n your wife."

"I ain't buyin' your idea," Mallick told the Los Angeles man. "I say the killer had a reason."

"How're we gonna find that reason?" scowled Rossiter. "He ain't about to oblige us by admittin' to it."

"Too bad," Sanders said dryly. "This would be a fine time for somebody to confess — and easier on our nerves."

They were silent a while, thinking, then Rossiter said gruffly, "You keep remindin' me I'm in charge. All right, here's a notion. It might help some if — uh — some jasper can't prove he didn't sneak out and knife the tinhorn."

"Does any one of us really have an alibi?" frowned Sanders.

"Me and Groot shared a shack, so we can vouch for each other," Rossiter declared. "Who else beside the tinhorn claimed a shack for himself?"

"We bunked in here," said Larry. "Sanders was here too, and we'd have roused for sure if he'd snuck out."

"My dear husband would never leave me during the night," Mrs Faber murmured with her eyes downcast.

"Who does that leave?" asked Mallick.

"Come now," protested Kolbe. "Surely I and the murder victim weren't the only ones who chose to be alone."

"There's only me," said the redhead. "I ain't about to confess to bein' a killer and it's for sure you won't, Big Shot, so that puts us back where we started — and gettin' nowhere."

"Somebody's lying," said Sanders.

"Uh huh," grunted Stretch. "Be kind of handy if we could guess who."

"None of us is safe!" fretted Mrs Faber.

"Courage, my dear," begged Faber.

"Maybe we're all safe now," suggested Chris. "I don't see any sport here that looks crazy, so whoever knifed Jerry had his reason, which don't mean he's got a reason for killin' again. He wanted Jerry, nobody else." She eyed Larry expectantly. "Any ideas, Big Boy?"

"Killer waited till it was dark and everybody sleepin'," mused Larry. "I can't read his mind on account of I don't know him, so how do we know he won't do it again?"

"You're about to make a point," guessed Sanders.

"Which is . . . ?" demanded Kolbe.

"We take no chances tonight," said Larry. "That means we take turns to sleep. Here and now, we'll decide who's gonna stand guard, or patrol this place, while the rest of us're bunked down."

"Shouldn't one guard be sufficient?"

asked the preacher.

"That one guard, wide awake while the rest of us're sleepin', could be the killer," Larry retorted.

"There should be two guards patrolling," said Sanders.

"Two-hour shifts startin' ten o'clock," nodded Larry. "Okay by you, Rossiter?"

"I guess," shrugged Rossiter.

"Still unsatisfactory," argued Kolbe. "What if the guards are in league — two of a kind? How many of us were acquainted when our journey began? This man and I . . . " He nodded to Sanders, "boarded the coach in Oklahoma. When four boarded at Quimera, we were strangers to one another, except for the reverend and his wife and the fact that the gambler and this young woman were casually acquainted."

"That's a valid point," Sanders conceded.

"My partner and me buddied up a long time ago," said Larry, matching stares with Rossiter and Mallick. Same with you two?" They nodded. "So how about this? First hitch, the preacher and the guard, second hitch, Mister Kolbe and the driver. It'll be two o'clock in the mornin' when they finish their shift. Then they come wake Sanders and me . . . "

"That'll leave your partner odd man out, so I got a better idea," interjected the redhead. "You rouse me and I'll stand guard with you till four. That'll make your partner and Mister Sanders the four till daylight guards."

"Look, you don't have to . . . " began Stretch.

"Tall man, I ain't helpless nor useless," she declared. "Any time your buddy with the muscles passes me, he won't find me with my eyes closed and snorin'. I can take my turn — and I'm *gonna*. We gonna waste time wranglin' about it?"

"Any objections, gentlemen?" asked Sanders. There were no protests. "Well, that seems to settle it. We work to the roster proposed by Lawrence."

"Startin' ten o'clock tonight, huh?" frowned Mallick.

"Ten o'clock," nodded Sanders. "And let's be optimistic. If the clearing operation at Fortuna Pass proceeds without mishap, we could hear from Deputy Covington by sundown tomorrow, which means there'll be no further need of guard duty."

"I must comply with the majority decision in this matter," muttered Kolbe.

"Do you have any reservations, Brother Kolbe?" enquired Faber.

"Just one cause for disquiet — the obvious cause," said Kolbe. "One of us will be on guard duty with a murderer."

Larry grimaced, but nodded agreement.

"Yeah. That's about the size of it."

"So I presume each pair will stay well separated," said Sanders. "Keeping an eye on each other as well as the camp. And this raises another question. Who among us is unarmed?"

Mallick chuckled softly, his eyes on Faber.

"Preachers don't tote guns, huh?"

"I am a man of peace and have never owned a firearm," said Faber.

"I hope nobody imagines *I'm* armed," snapped Kolbe.

"We'll have enough hardware," shrugged Larry. "Preacher, like it or not, you'll be totin' my full-loaded Winchester, and Mister Kolbe can borrow my partner's."

"We're forgetting your fellow-sentry, Lawrence," said Sanders.

"I got a pistol," Chris curtly announced. "It ain't real big and don't nobody ask where I carry it. What matters is it'll pop loud enough if I have to use it."

"All right now, everybody savvy which shift they'll be workin'?" challenged Rossiter.

"I don't reckon anybody's forgot already," said the redhead. "Preacher and the guard ten till midnight, Big Shot and the driver midnight to two,

Handsome and me two to four, Mister Sanders and the beanpole four till sunrise."

"Well," said Mallick, "I guess that's all settled."

"Anybody else got somethin' to say?" prodded Rossiter.

"Yeah, me." said Larry, rising. "Somethin' else better be decided, but the ladies ain't in on it. We'd best parley about it outside while they . . . "

"Wash the dishes, clean up in the kitchen, woman chores," said Chris. "I'm way ahead of you, Big Boy. Well — *ma'am*? What're we waitin' for?"

Larry led the men from the saloon to the well-house, a position out of earshot of the saloon. They gathered around to listen, and what he had to say was said flatly, in tones that invited no argument.

"Gets cooler here, but not till late at night, stays hot through the day. Forty-eight hours the deputy told you. Maybe

92

they'll clear the pass by then, and maybe not, so we can't delay puttin' the tinhorn six feet underground. It's just somethin' has to be done."

"Some prospectors left stuff behind," said Stretch. "Not much, but enough. We found a spade and a pickax we can use."

"My partner and me're volunteerin' to be grave-diggers," offered Larry. "Only we got another chore first."

"Meanin' what?" demanded Mallick.

"Arville's clothes and his bag have to be searched," said Larry. "Anybody know if he had kin? No, I guess not. So we look for somethin', a letter or some other paper that'll tell us . . ."

"If he has a relative who should be advised of his death," nodded Sanders. "Yes, I'm sure we all understand."

"Then there's whatever cash he was totin'," Larry pointed out. "So we all search, okay? And it ought to be done right now."

"Yes," winced Kolbe. "If we must."

They returned to the shack wherein

the gambler had met his end. The Texans conducted the search, the other men watching. Clothing and valise yielded two spare shirts, some celluloid collars, a change of underwear, $75 and small change, a watch, some cigars and toothpicks and a box of matches, handkerchiefs, two decks of cards, one with its wrapper intact, a Remington derringer and six spare bullets for it. There was a piece of mail, just one letter addressed to the dead man care of a Quimera hotel. Larry passed it to Faber.

"More fittin' if you read it, I reckon."

Faber extracted and unfolded the single sheet, read for a few moments, then offered the gist of it.

"From the poor man's sister in Santa Fe, a Mrs G. Rawley. Her greeting is 'Dear Brother Jerome.' The lady writes that her husband's drygoods store is prospering and urges her brother to abandon the life of a drifting gambler and resettle in her hometown. Her husband was willing to employ him and teach him the business."

"So now we know to whom his personal effects should be sent," said Sanders. "With, of course, a letter informing her of her loss."

"Runt, we don't have to plant him in just that blanket," suggested Stretch. "Couple shacks're fallin' apart. We could find enough planks to fix some kind of . . ."

"Sure," nodded Larry. "We'll do that."

"I will conduct a funeral service," insisted Faber. "And all should attend."

"We'll all be there," Rossiter assured him. "It's for sure nobody's lettin' any other jasper out of his sight."

The grave was dug beside those of the old miners who had died here. At 11 a.m., the mortal remains of Jerome Arville were laid to rest after a short eulogy from the preacher and the reading of psalms from his bible, his wife weeping softly, Chris Brodie leading the singing of 'Rock Of Ages.'

After the burial, Dora Faber kept up her moaning and sighing, much to the irritation of a hot-tempered redhead.

"Who d'you think you are — chief mourner?" snapped Chris. "Why, you scarce *knew* the poor slob!"

"*Really*, Sister Brodie," chided Faber.

"Don't 'Sister Brodie' me!" flared Chris. "I'm fed to my teeth with her whinin'!"

The other woman suddenly showed spirit.

"You are heartless and — and you have no imagination!" she accused the redhead. "The question that troubles me, terrifies me, is who will be *next* to die?"

"Now, Mrs Faber . . . " began Sanders.

"What if you're wrong?" she challenged. "Does it *have* to be one of us killed that poor man? Can you be absolutely sure there's nobody else here?"

"Couldn't be, ma'am," frowned Larry. "My partner and me been here most of

96

a week before you folks showed up and we ain't seen nobody else."

"Checked every shack soon as we got here," offered Stretch.

"Wait!" Kolbe said tensely. They were outside the saloon now, he staring across to the mound. "Those tunnels . . . "

"Boarded up," shrugged Stretch.

"Did you think to investigate them?" asked Kolbe. "For all you know, one of them could be the killer's hiding place. You haven't seen him because he doesn't show himself during the day. But — perhaps — at *night* . . . !"

"I suppose, if those shafts haven't been searched, they should be," said Sanders.

"But they may not be safe," Faber said nervously.

"I positively refuse to venture into any of them," said Kolbe. "I am not ashamed to admit to a fear of being buried alive."

"We'll talk about it while we eat," suggested Larry.

"I can take a hint," shrugged Chris.

During that makeshift lunch, Larry's sixth sense plagued him. He couldn't shake his conviction there would be other deaths in this place.

4

Dodging the Grim Reaper

NOTHING like a murder to jar the nerves of nine people confined to one room, even a bar room. Sanders noted the change, though he refrained from comment. Last night and this morning, at supper and breakfast, the group was scattered, some seated at tables drawn together, the others squatting with backs to the bar or over by the batwings or in a corner. Now the tables were separated and the men squatting on the floor forming a semi-circle. For the obvious reason. They were watching one another, no man turning his back on the others.

Kolbe grudgingly accepted that they were eating regularly, at the same time complaining of the monotony of the fare — jackrabbit was not to his taste and that went double for beans. Chris reminded him that nine people, most of them with healthy appetites, tended to deplete what provisions were available. This led the taller Texan to remark, "We all better be partial to fish. That's the only chow we ain't apt to run short of and, right after we check them old shafts, my partner and me gonna ride to the creek again and catch as many as'll jump to our bait."

"We should not complain," murmured the preacher's wife. "Fish is nourishing food."

"Gettin' short, are we?" Larry roused from his reverie and aimed this question at the redhead.

"I used up most of your canned stuff," she told him. "Like we keep remindin' ourselves, we got no guarantee it'll be a fast job — clearin' the pass."

"Well," he shrugged. "Long as the fish're jumpin'."

"You'll just ride out," Mallick said with a hint of accusation.

"That's right," said Larry, staring hard at him. "What's your gripe, Mallick? Afraid we won't come back? Listen, we won't be takin' our saddlebags, packrolls either, and you never saw the day we'd leave our gear behind, not if we figured to run out on this party."

"If we ain't objectin' to you hombres wanderin' east or west for a little huntin'," drawled Stretch, "you oughtn't care about us headin' for the creek to fish."

"We might do that," shrugged Rossiter.

"But first you'll search the tunnels?" frowned Faber. "Is it possible — some person we've not seen — could be in hiding, as Dora fears?"

"Won't know till we take a look, preacher," said Larry.

"We may not need to check all three shafts," offered Sanders.

"We?" prodded Stretch. "You plan on helpin' us?"

"Shouldn't I?" challenged Sanders.

"I don't doubt you wanderers have seen the insides of many a mine shaft, but don't forget I'm better qualified in such matters. Tunnels of every type, railroad tunnels through mountains and mine shafts, excavations of all kinds, are one of my specialties. Yes, I'd better be with you."

"You said we mightn't have to check all three shafts," Larry reminded him.

"Well, it'll depend, won't it?" suggested Sanders. "First we'll examine the boarded-up shaft-heads, find out how firmly they're fixed. If, for instance, we discover one entrance can be forced open from inside — movable boards would indicate that . . . "

"That'd be a possible hideaway," nodded Larry. "Yeah, I savvy."

"I guess we'll move around back of the ground, climb up top too," said Stretch. "Lookin' for an outlet?"

"Certainly," said Sanders. "It has to be a thorough check. No use overlooking possibilities."

After lunch, the gathering began

breaking up. The Texans loath to take chances, slipped their holster-thongs, unbuckled their sidearms and left them in the redhead's care.

"If we get into a shaft, there could be loose earth, plenty dust," Larry explained.

"Enough to clog our irons," said Stretch. "Too much dirt gets into a hogleg, it don't work so good. And, when we have to use 'em . . ."

"You need to be sure they're gonna work right," she nodded. "Sure. I understand."

"Mind keeping an eye on mine also?" Sanders politely requested, proffering his .38.

"You're so all-fire mannerly, Mister Sanders," she remarked. "How could a girl say no?" As the three men began leaving, she called after them softly, "Take care, boys."

While Larry and the engineer made for the first shafthead, Stretch trudged around the mound. Along the base, all the way to the rear and the north side, he searched for but failed to locate an outlet from any of the shafts. He was climbing up top when Larry and Sanders reached the first tunnelmouth and studied the boards.

"Nailed securely," said Sanders, tugging at them. "And too many of them to leave an aperture. You'll note there isn't space enough between any of them for a man to squeeze through."

"So, 'less there's another way out . . ."

"Exactly. Now let's check the next one."

They were leery of what they found at the entrance to the second shaft. No openings, but the boards were loose. Without effort, Larry pulled two of them away. They peered into the gloom beyond, then traded glances.

"Well, not impossible — we've established that much," said Sanders. "This one we'll have to check, after we take a look at Shaft Number Three."

The entrance to the third shaft was as secure as the first. They returned to the centre opening just as Stretch clambered down to join them and report, "No other ways out. All round or up top. I even lifted a rock or two."

"So this tunnel warrants investigation," decided Sanders. "We'll need a light and — ah, our fire-haired friend, how she reads my mind."

Chris had quit the saloon and was coming toward them, toting a lamp.

"Found a spare," she called. "Made sure there's oil enough in the tank and the wick primed." Pausing, passing the lamp to Sanders, she stared past him. "Sure is *dark* in there."

"Ain't that the truth," agreed Stretch.

"What d'you think you'll find?" she demanded.

"Quien sabe?" shrugged Larry. "Ask us when we come out."

"Watch yourselves," she cautioned. "Be sure you do come out."

Sanders raised the funnel and turned up the wick. Larry scratched a match and, when the lamp was working, followed Sanders into the shaft with

Stretch at his heels. Chris wasn't the only interested observer. Kolbe watched from over by the wellhouse, smoking a Havana, the Fabers from the doorway of their cabin.

Seven yards into the shaft, holding the lamp high and keeping his eyes busy, Sanders warned, "We should tread carefully — and slowly."

"And look for sign," muttered Stretch. "Bones, empty cans, blankets maybe, anything to show some hombre holed up in here."

"I ain't spotted footprints," said Larry. "Sanders, you don't like it in here?"

"Not one little bit," the engineer quietly complained, as they moved a few feet deeper into the tunnel. "This could've been the first shaft they bored, and they worked too fast for my liking. Some of the shoring has deteriorated — they were too hasty in choosing their lumber. Woodville, you're the tallest of us. Take the lamp. Hold it high."

"Gotcha," grunted Stretch.

"Voices low," begged Sanders, while leading them another ten feet. "Step carefully. Sudden noise could cause vibration. If you want me to be frank . . . "

"Yeah," said Larry. "We'd like that."

"I'm becoming edgy, uncertain of what we're getting into," Sanders confided.

"Well . . . " Stretch winced uneasily, "that makes two of us, and I don't reckon my buddy's having fun neither."

Sanders raised his eyes as he took two more steps. Again, he felt disquiet. The shaft's beamed ceiling bothered him, too many crossbeams askew, tending to sag.

"Are you two . . . ?" he began.

"We're still lookin' for sign," muttered Larry. "And we ain't seein' nothin' to show . . . "

He didn't finish his reply. Sander's action was so swift that he was taken off-guard. The instant his ears caught the danger signal, a subdued grinding, splintering sound, the engineer whirled and threw himself against him, tackling him while he was off-balance and throwing both of them a full four feet backward. Simultaneously, Sanders gasped a command to Stretch.

"Back out!"

Larry had been forced clear of a danger spot. As he lurched to his feet with Sanders gripping his right arm, his blood ran cold. A section above where he had been standing seconds before, *exactly* where he had stood, had given way. Beams were cracking and rock and rubble coming down. He turned with Sanders and, en route to the shafthead, glanced back. The tunnel shook from the impact of heavy stuff hitting its floor, rock, earth, rubble, so much of it that, in a matter of moments, the top of the pile was close to the ceiling.

They backed out into the sunlight, sweating, followed by a cloud of dust. Stretch muttered a curse and extinguished the lamp. Pallid, shuddering, Sanders retreated a few paces and fished out a kerchief to mop his brow. Larry stood beside him, eyeing him intently.

"I'm in the business — it's my profession," the engineer said shakily. "But — the risks — the danger — you never get used to it — even after long experience. Look at me — I can't stop trembling . . . !"

"I'm lookin'," said Larry. "Lookin' at the man just now saved my life. I'd be under the mess in there, if you hadn't shoved me clear. Sanders, I'd feel real bad if it turned out you're the killer here."

"I'd feel just as bad," mumbled Sanders.

The others, alerted by the din from inside the shaft, were converging on them. First to reach them was the redhead, who took the lamp from Stretch and stared hard at Sanders. Kolbe and the stage crew demanded to be told what had happened.

"Something terrible," fretted the preacher's wife.

"Better you should ask what *nearly* happened," sighed Larry, slapping dust from his clothes with his Stetson.

"My compadre durn near got buried in there," Stretch told everybody. "Roof started cavin' in — and he was right under it. Wasn't for Sanders, he'd *still* be under it — meanin' a ton or more of rock."

Larry tried to address Dora Faber politely; it called for quite an effort.

"We're obliged to you, ma'am, for your notion a loco killer could be hid in a shaft, but we found no sign of life in there and it's for sure he ain't in the other two."

"Dora, my dear, you've nothing to reproach yourself for," said Faber. "Our brave brothers did volunteer to make a search."

"Well, sure." Stretch shrugged uncomfortably. "Ain't nobody's fault."

"I think," said Sanders, turning toward the saloon. "I need to rest."

"C'mon, hero," frowned Chris, falling in beside him. "You look beat — like

110

you've been eyeball to eyeball with Death."

"Believe me, I feel exactly as I appear to you," he declared.

Larry donned his hat and stood arms akimbo, trading stares with the other men.

"What will you do now?" demanded Kolbe.

"Don't know about the rest of you," said Larry. "But my partner and me're goin' fishin'."

"I'll saddle up for us," offered Stretch, "while you go collect our hardware."

The Los Angeles man stood with Faber and the stage crew, Mrs Faber having gone back to the shack she shared with the preacher. The four watched Stretch emerge from the barn leading his and his partner's saddled mounts, and Larry coming back from the saloon wearing his sidearm, Stretch's double-holstered belt hung over his left arm.

Joining Stretch, he waited for him

to strap on his weapons. They then swung astride and nudged their animals to movement, making for the brush south of the ghost town. It was then, staring after them, that Kolbe grimly declared, "I don't trust those two. From the start, I've had grave doubts about them."

"Charity, Brother Kolbe," protested Faber. "They show true concern for our welfare."

"I call that lulling us into a false sense of security, a ploy to distract us," retorted Kolbe.

"Somethin' special you don't like about 'em?" drawled Mallick.

"They are uncouth, ruffianly and presumptuous," complained Kolbe. "For a couple of shiftless wanderers, it seems to me they're too heavily armed. Who among us can really trust them?"

"I try to trust all men," Faber said virtuously.

"Got to admit *I'm* a mite leery of 'em," muttered Rossiter. "Mister Kolbe might have the right idea about 'em."

Larry's nerves had stopped jumping when, some time later, he and his partner rode out of the brush and on to the creek's bank and the fishing spot now familiar to them. They dismounted, ground-reined their animals, broke out their lines, baited their hooks and cast them into the stream, then squatted side by side.

Stretch held both lines while Larry built two cigarettes.

"Close, runt," he quietly remarked.

"Damn right," breathed Larry. "Give me a choice, that ain't the way I'd want to go."

"You wouldn't've smothered," opined Stretch. "First big rock to hit you would've mashed your head."

"Ain't that the truth," agreed Larry.

He scratched a match on a thumbnail, lit both quirleys, nudged one into his partner's mouth and took his line. Stretch felt a tug a few moments later, hauled his catch out, used his jack-knife, then recast.

We ain't had much chance to parley

private since company arrived," he remarked. "Some nervous deal, huh? One of them nice folks put a knife in the gamblin' man. I can't guess who did it and neither can you."

"That's the hell of it," grouched Larry. "I keep thinkin' about 'em all, but . . . "

"No hunches?"

"Nope. Nary a notion."

"That irks you."

"You know it."

"Runt, your brain always was smarter'n mine, but I get ideas once in a while. This idea ain't much help, but it's the only one I got."

"So let me hear it."

"Wasn't neither of them females. I can't figure a preacher's wife sneakin' through the dark and into that shack to stab the tinhorn."

"And the strawberry roan filly?"

"Not her neither. What d'you say?"

Larry grinned wryly.

"She ain't the type," he said. "A real hardnose with a chip on her shoulder,

114

but I'd never be nervous of havin' my back to her. One thing she ain't is sneaky."

"Sure," nodded Stretch. "Speaks her mind, talks straight. Had to be a man did it, so how d'you figure 'em."

"Can't point a finger at any of 'em," muttered Larry. "I don't want it to be Sanders, so maybe I ain't thinkin' clear about him. The preacher and the big shot from Los Angeles — forget 'em. And the stage crew? Regular stage line men, just a couple more workin' stiffs." He hauled in an easy catch, but that couldn't cheer him. "Most times I get a feelin' in my bones, but not this time."

"You're only human, amigo," Stretch consoled him. "You can't guess 'em all."

"Got a mean feelin', but not in my bones," complained Larry. "Its in my head and givin' me hell."

"What?" prodded Stretch.

"Somethin' got by me," frowned Larry. "I'm missin' somethin'."

115

"Look, every other son's as mixed up as you," shrugged Stretch. "All of 'em — 'cept the killer. He knows why he butchered Arville. Nobody else does."

"If I could guess the why of it — *why* Arville was killed — that'd help some," said Larry. "Red didn't know him real close but, to her, he didn't seem like a hombre some sonofabitch'd want to put a knife in."

"Trouble is," said Stretch, "this killer's liable to go free. When the deputy from San Raphael comes to Midas Mound, he'll be tellin' them travellers they can get through the pass. Then they'll up and leave, make San Raphael the day after that coach rolls out."

"The deputy'll be told about the killin'," mused Larry. "He'll report it to the sheriff and the passengers and crew'll answer all his questions and he'll end up no wiser'n me."

"That irks you too," guessed Stretch. "You'd as soon get to the gizzard of it and nail the killer before the deputy shows."

"We've been around killers many a time," Larry reminded him. "Mostly, we've known who we got to be leery of. This time it's different. We *don't* know."

"I'm just rememberin' what that Kolbe feller said," winced Stretch. "Tonight, from around ten o'clock to sun-up when we're standin' guard, one of us'll be with that lousy killer."

Realizing they'd solve no mysteries by further discussion, they looked to their fishing. A formidable catch, enough for supper and breakfast, was slung to their horses when, in the late afternoon, they headed back to the ghost town.

★ ★ ★

While Chris Brodie was preparing the evening meal with help from Stretch, three men squatted by a cookfire in a grove some distance south of San Raphael, satisfied their hunger and awaited the return of one Al McGrail. A picketline had been rigged. To it were tied seven saddle animals, most of them geldings, strong-limbed and, when needs be, capable of speed.

The three by the fire were Griff Arno, Cass Elkin and Philo Rolfe, three roughly garbed men whose sidearms were housed in tied-down holsters. They traded an occasional remark, but softly, keeping their ears cocked. How soon before their scout rejoined them?

That question was answered a few minutes later. Subdued hoofbeats announced the return of bulky, flat-nosed McGrail. Automatically, Arno reached for a plate and filled it from the pan.

McGrail rode in and dismounted. Muttered greetings were exchanged as he tied his horse. Then, as he accepted his share of their austere supper, he dug a fork into it and announced, "No use us waitin' for Blystone in town. Stage mightn't arrive tomorrow at all." He ate for a while, his cronies waxing impatient, but holding back on their questions. "I learned all about it in San Raphael. Easy chore. Like Blystone always says, all you have to do is loiter here and there and just listen."

"Sure," nodded Elkin. "So what d'you know?"

"Whole bunch of toilers usin' their muscles at Fortuna Pass, workin' shifts, gettin' ready to use dynamite too," said McGrail. "Avalanche. No way the stage could make San Raphael, but nobody found out about the pile-up till after the stage left Quimera."

"*More* waitin'," scowled Rolfe.

"Somethin' else Blystone always says," Arno reminded him. "Waitin' is safer. Worst time for dividin' the loot is right after you've grabbed it. Better to wait till things cool down."

"I'll allow we got a smart boss and he ain't yet steered us wrong," muttered Elkin. "But, this time, I'm as impatient as Philo. Ain't that I don't trust Blystone. I just hanker to feel my share snug in my pockets."

119

"You got more to tell us, Al," guessed Arno. "What else did you hear? Stage turned back to Quimera?"

"They could've turned back, but they didn't," said McGrail. "The San Raphael sheriff sent a deputy to ride round the mountains and head 'em off before they started the long climb to the pass."

"And he did that?" asked Arno.

"Uh huh," grunted McGrail. "He's back in town now. I heard him talkin' it around."

"If that stage didn't head back to Quimera, where is it?" demanded Rolfe.

"And Blystone," growled Elkin. "And the seventy-five thousand?"

"Ever hear of a ghost town, Midas Mound?" grinned McGrail. "I figure we could find it if we head straight east from here."

He continued eating, and talking. His companions listened to all he had learned in San Raphael, the decision by the westbound passengers to await word of the clearing of the pass in a recently abandoned mine camp offering ample shelter, and his suggestion that they should join their leader at Midas Mound rather than wait for him in San Raphael. He had finished eating and was swigging coffee when Arno asked,

"Why, Al? He won't be expectin' us. And you know how he is. When Jarvis Blystone gives an order . . . "

"He'll be runnin' out of patience," opined McGrail. "We'll be a welcome sight when we show up with the horses."

"I guess even a jasper as cold-nerved as Blystone could run out of patience," frowned Rolfe.

"Well, let's try readin' his mind right now," drawled McGrail. "He's stuck and he can't be sure for how long. Nothin's for sure. The deputy said it. Risky situation at the pass. It'd take forty-eight hours to clear it, but the work-crews ain't gonna bet their lives on that, specially the dynos from Sun Flats that have to plant the charges — hopin' they won't start *another* rockfall."

"So?" prodded Elkin.

"So this way Blystone gets a third choice," explained McGrail. "We show up, ride into Midas Mound with spare horses and wantin' to be helpful, offering to take him to wherever he was headed, but not lettin' on we know him or he knows us."

"You could be right," reflected Arno. "Yeah, he'd likely appreciate it."

"Ghost town couldn't be all that cosy," remarked Elkin.

"And Blystone's a feller sure relishes his comforts," Rolfe pointed out. "Good chow, high class liquor, the best cigars. Seems to me, by the time we get there, he'll be glad to shake the dust of Midas Mound off his duds."

They debated McGrail's suggestion for some minutes, after which Arno asked him, "Think we could find the place?"

"It's southwest of the stage route,"

said McGrail. "I'm sure enough, if we head out now and keep pushin' east, we'll find it before the work gangs've cleared the pass."

"Yeah, all right," said Arno, rising. "So let's get started."

The cooking gear was stashed. Elkin killed the fire with earth and joined his companeros in readying the horses. The four were moving eastward soon afterward, each leading a saddled animal.

Back in Quimera, around 9 p.m., Deputy Mike Harrow ran his boss to ground in the Full Hand Saloon. The sheriff was drinking alone, preferring to be sole occupant of a table by the south wall, till Harrow bought a beer, brought it to the table and seated himself. He took an envelope from a pants pocket and placed it before his chief.

"Just collected it at the Western Union office. Wire for you from Sheriff Lunceford at San Raphael."

"Hope it's better news this time,"

muttered Winters. He set his glass aside, tore the envelope and extracted and read the message. Frowning, he remarked, "I appreciate Earl Lunceford keeping me informed, but I wish he had better news."

"Hey, I got two cousins and a few friends workin' claims at Sun Flats," frowned Harrow. "For all I know, they could've volunteered for that dirty chore. Hasn't been more trouble, has there? Anybody hurt?"

"You can stop worrying about your cousins and buddies," shrugged the sheriff. "If they're helping at the pass, well, there haven't been casualties. What Earl's telling me is progress is slow. There was another rockfall. Fortunately everybody was well clear. So there'll be a lot more rubble to be hauled out and, so far, the explosives boys aren't even *thinking* of planting charges."

"Maybe they never will," suggested Harrow, after half-emptying his tankard. "Too big a risk. Fortuna Pass ain't wide, and those rockwalls're steep and high."

"I just hope they're getting all the food they need, Mike," said Winters.

"Stage passengers waitin' at Midas Mound you mean?" asked the deputy.

"I don't mean the bunch at the pass," growled Winters. "You can bet those diggers provisioned up before they left Sun Flats. Never was a mine-hand didn't have a big appetite."

"Stage crew'll take good care of the passengers," Harrow assured him. "Eli says he's hunted and fished that piece of territory and the huntin's good. By now, the driver or the guard've downed antelope or quail, enough of it to keep the folks eatin'."

"So chances are they won't starve," said Winters. "But, man oh man, some of em'll be out of patience by now I'm thinking. Lorin Powell told me about 'em. You know a rich businessman name of Kolbe's with those people? Lorin says he's a mighty important gent in his hometown, Los Angeles.

Well, think about that, Mike. *He* won't take kindly to conditions at Midas Mound."

"Probably sue the stage line," grinned Harrow. "How about the others?"

"Some kind of engineer bound for Arizona," said Winters. "He'd be used to roughing it. Jerry Arville — remember him? I don't guess he'd be in a hurry to get wherever he's going. A preacher and his wife, well, they'll likely make the most of it."

"And Chris Brodie," remarked Harrow. "Salty Chris, tough gal who can handle herself in any fix — except when Old Ma Hapthorne gets her bustle in a bind, her and her do-good friends."

The sheriff finished his drink, cursed softly and lit a cigar.

"Reformers," he said in disgust. "Bunch of old hypocrites. Jealousy's the real reason they ran the redhead out of town. Not that Lucius Hapthorne helped any, what with his hanging around Chris all the time — damn

126

fool. Old enough to be the girl's father. Ought to know better. Big Bessie and her friends can't abide any woman younger and prettier than they ever were." He gazed around the bar-room and heaved a sigh. "Confidentially, I miss her."

"Not the way Mayor Hapthorne's missin' her," guessed Harrow.

"Hell, no," said Winters. "But she brightened up this place."

"Bright is right," said Harrow. "She's a gal sure wears colorful rigouts. And that red hair of hers."

"Sang real sweet and always good for a laugh," recalled Winters. "No real harm in her. Kept the customers happy. Why, this used to be the happiest bar in Quimera, but look at it now. It reminds me of when there's a death in the family."

"She'll make out," Harrow assured him. "Quimera's the loser. Next saloonkeeper hires her, he won't regret it, that's for sure. She'll draw a lot of trade."

"I wonder how the other passengers're making out," mused Winters. "Stuck at Midas Mound."

Chris Brodie and the other travellers were, at this time, calling it a day, all save Faber and the shotgun guard, scheduled to begin guard duty at 10 o'clock. Faber and Mallick were in conversation a short distance from the shack in which Dora Faber was bedding down. Kolbe and Rossiter had left the saloon. The Texans were breaking out their bedrolls and the redhead making for the batwings when Sanders, now recovered from his brush with Death in Shaft Number 2, rose and followed her.

5

The Accusation

SHE had draped a canary-yellow shawl over her head and shoulders and was a few yards from the saloon, her keen ears catching soft footsteps behind her. Turning quickly, she at once recognized the engineer. He gestured reassuringly and nodded to the wellhouse; they moved over there to talk.

"You ought to get some sleep," she advised.

"You too, Miss Brodie," he said, lighting a cigar. "Don't worry, I won't keep you long. This is my last cigar. I just felt like talking."

"Still jumpy I bet," she frowned. "Bad scare, huh?"

"While it lasted," he said. "My nerves are steady now. Good fish supper works wonders. My compliments on your cooking."

"Lucky for us the fishin's good," she shrugged. "By now, Mister Big Shot Kolbe's likely cravin' a thick steak with all the trimmin's, big fancy supper like he eats in Los Angeles, some high class hash-house in the big city. Might be some of the others'll start grouchin' soon. Some sports *always* complain, never settle for what they got. Hell, fish beats no chow at all."

"Yes, I agree," he said. "Look, if you didn't trust me, we wouldn't be having this private conversation, would we?"

"Well," she said. "I can't see you doin' poor Jerry with a knife."

"Nor I you," he said. "So, since we trust each other, do you mind a few questions? I mean personal questions."

"Personal?" she challenged. "What would a gent like you want to know about the likes of me?"

"Well, for instance, what will you do when we reach San Raphael?" he asked.

"There'll be plenty saloons there," she said. "Any town with saloons — and I never yet saw a town didn't have — I can earn a few bucks singin' to the trade or hustlin' sports to the gamblin' tables for a percentage of what the house takes 'em for."

"You're young," he observed. "Just about of age, I'd guess."

"You'd guess wrong. I'm twenty-five."

"You don't look it. Tell me, haven't you ever wanted to do better for yourself?"

"For me, there's never nothin' better. I've been goin' it alone since I was fifteen. Hell! That's ten years."

"Quite a coincidence," he remarked. "My parents died when I was that age, but I had other relatives, uncles and aunts who took me in and financed my studies. Thanks to them, I'm a qualified engineer with a lot of experience behind me."

"So you were lucky, Mister Sanders," she said. "That's how it goes, huh?

Some're lucky and some ain't. You just got to play the hand that's dealt you."

"It's been rough for you," he surmised.

"I've done it all," she declared. "Hustled dishes in greasy spoon joints, took in other folks' washin', but mostly I've worked saloons. Only places I ain't worked is cat-houses."

"No matter how difficult things became for you," he said thoughtfully, "you held back from becoming a joy-girl."

"Give it the right name," she said flatly. "Whore. They ain't never gonna make a whore of me."

"Have you considered marriage?" he asked.

"No respectable jasper'd want me for a wife," she said. "Only the riff raff, the kind that don't bother about a gold band or a weddin' paper."

"Here's where I risk a slapped face — or maybe a fist in my eye," he said gingerly.

"Go ahead," she invited. "Take the risk. It couldn't be any more dangerous than what damn near happened in that old mine shaft."

"All right, I'll take a chance," he decided. "Just keep this thought in mind. I don't mean to offend you. I make this suggestion out of interest in what's to become of you, your future, when we're gone from this place."

"So?" she prodded.

"You could improve yourself," he told her. "Any person can be better than what they've been. The way you speak, for instance. Any schoolteacher could give you a few pointers, teach you correct speech, and it mightn't be as difficult as you'd imagine. And any older woman running a ladies' store or just working there could advise you about the right kind of clothes, choice of colors and style. Miss Brodie, you don't *have* to go on being a saloon-woman. By improving yourself, you could end up being a saleslady with a regular salary, enough to support yourself. If

133

you have the *will* to break free, make something of yourself, nobody can stop you." He shrugged apologetically. "Sorry. I've never done this before. I am taking liberties and you've every right to be angry."

She decided, after a thoughtful silence,

"No, I ain't mad at you."

"You *aren't* mad at me," he corrected. "Try that for starters, saying aren't instead of ain't. See how easy it can be? You're bright. There's plenty of good sense under that fire-red hair of yours."

"All I know about you is you're an engineer with a lot of education," she murmured. "That all you'll say of yourself? You got a wife — kids?"

"I'm older than you by six years and I'm single," he said. "Ever since I graduated, I've been too caught up in my work to form an attachment for any woman."

"Like that, huh?" she reflected. "All work and no playin' around.

Well, okay, Mister Sanders, I've never thought much about changin' my ways, but maybe I'll remember what you've said. Guess it's worth thinkin' about. And I'm obliged. This was real friendly of you."

"My pleasure," he said politely. "But, if we're friends now, I do have a first name. It's Whitney — Whit for short."

"Fine by me, Whit," she smiled. "My first name's Christine — Chris for short. 'Night, Whit."

"Goodnight, Chris," he said.

He stayed by the well watching, thinking about her, till she was lost from view, then moved back into the saloon to catch up on his sleep.

At 10 p.m. all but Mallick and the preacher were asleep. The first guards began their stint, the next two hours passing without incident. Roused by Faber and Mallick respectively, the Los Angeles man and the driver took over at midnight, Kolbe reacted unfavorably to broken sleep, but managed to stay awake until 2 a.m.

He saw Rossiter wave wearily and trudge to the shack he shared with Mallick.

"Very co-operative of you, driver, I don't think," he reflected. "Leaving me to wake that insolent bawd and the rough-neck Lawrence."

He was relieved, but did not think to express gratitude, when the redhead emerged from her quarters and moved toward him.

"You go bed down again, Big Shot," she invited. "I ain't — I mean I am not squeamish about rousin' my partner-guard."

"I'm sure you wouldn't be," he loftily retorted before moving away.

She made for the saloon. Just as she reached the batwings, they swung outward and Larry appeared, wearing his poncho, touching his hat-brim to her.

"Right on time, Red," he drawled, as they stepped clear of the building.

"That's me," she shrugged. "Always on time."

"Okay now," he said. "You just loiter some and keep your purty eyes peeled. I'll get back to you in a little while."

"What'll you be doin'?" she demanded.

"Gonna climb the mound," he told her. "Want to take a look at the land hereabouts. Might get lucky, Red. If I sight a rider, he could be the deputy from San Raphael on his way to tell you folks you can get movin' again."

"I got a feelin' it's too early," she said.

"A hunch, huh?" he prodded.

He imitated his partner's action of early afternoon the day before. Climbing the mound, he took his time, feeling no need of haste. Then, from up top, he scanned the surrounding terrain. What did he hope to see? Well, a pinpoint of light in the distance would mark the location of a campfire by which the San Raphael deputy was sleeping. He watched for some time, but saw nothing.

After descending, he joined the

redhead a short distance from the southernmost shack.

"Nothin'," she guessed.

"Nothin'," he said. "You want to kill time by talkin', that's okay. Long as we talk soft, we won't rouse the others." He hunkered and fished out his makings. "So how goes it with you? You cosy enough where you are?"

"I manage," she said. "I always manage."

"Great fish cookin', Red," he congratulated her. "We're sure obliged."

"You and your partner, some of the others, but not all of 'em," she murmured. "We're some mixture, huh? I got to tell you, Big Boy. Mister Important Kolbe's a horse's neck, and them Fabers give me a pain too."

"It takes all kinds," he suggested.

"I got nothin' against religion," she confided. "I've run into a cheerful priest or two in my time, and nuns that ain't — that aren't afraid to laugh. But I can't abide the gloomy ones like them Fabers, the kind that figure every girl workin' a saloon's got to be a whore."

"Don't let 'em rile you," he soothed. "Tell you what, Red. Try ignorin' 'em. Sometimes that's the only way. Just stay close-mouthed and pretend you don't hear."

He lit his cigarette and she squatted beside him, wrapping her arms about her knees.

"Close-mouthed, huh?" she prodded. "So you're a man don't call all women gabby?"

"Sure," he nodded. "My partner and me, we've known many a woman knew when to keep her mouth shut. We admire 'em for that."

"You do?" she challenged with a grin. "So start admirin' *me*, Larry Valentine." He coughed on half-inhaled smoke and mumbled something unintelligible, winning a soft chuckle from her. "Relax, trouble-shooter. Nobody else knows. I'm the only one pegged you and your buddy when we climbed out of the coach here, remembered you from newspaper pictures."

"Them pictures," he scowled.

"Lawrence and Woodville you called yourselves," she said. "Fine. I ain't dumb. Rightaway I figured you'd as soon nobody knows you're what you are, a couple outlaw-fighters with one helluva reputation. Don't fret yourself. I didn't let on to the others, not even to Whit Sanders, and I trust him like I trust you and your buddy."

"Appreciate that, Red," he said softly.

"In my line of work, a girl hears things," she said. "A whiskey drummer once told me you're quite a detective, good as any Pinkerton, so now I'm bettin' you crave to nail the skunk with the knife, him that killed Jerry Arville."

"Well," he shrugged. "Nine of us stuck here, one of us a killer, makes a plumb nervous situation. You bet I want him. But I can't read minds."

"Not even a hunch?" she asked.

"Nothin'," he complained. "Brain's

slowin' down maybe. You'd better believe the beanpole and me ain't as young as we were in the pictures you've seen."

"You could've fooled me," she said, patting his shoulder. "If the Lone Star Hellions're over the hill, nobody knows it."

He dribbled smoke through his nose and remarked, "It's good there's somebody else you trust. I mean, as well as Stretch and me."

"Meanin' Whit Sanders?"

"Meanin' him."

"You ain't — aren't leery of him?"

"I *oughtn't* be. He saved my life. If he wasn't so fast on his feet, I'd never've walked out of that shaft. So I owe him, and I'd hate to feel beholden to a killer."

"Not your first close call."

"Nope. But scarey, Red. Gettin' buried alive wouldn't be a barrel of fun."

When his cigarette was smoked down, Larry flicked the stub away

141

and got to his feet. Chris rose with him, asking, "We should keep movin' around?"

"Uh huh," he grunted. "Better we split up. You see or hear anything spooks you, you know what to do. Just holler, and I'll come a 'runnin'."

It seemed a slow two hours. At 4 o'clock, when they were sauntering toward the saloon, she told him she would sleep another two hours, then make for the kitchen to rustle up breakfast.

He roused his partner and the engineer and reported all quiet.

"Which ain't no guarantee it'll *stay* quiet," Stretch warned Sanders. "So we got to stay sharp, okay?"

"You can count on me to keep my eyes open and my ears cocked," declared Sanders. "I'm not about to forget that sporting man."

Larry dozed until he heard the batwings squeak on their rusting hinges. As the redhead passed him on her way to the kitchen, he sat up and squinted at his watch. 6 o'clock. Slow footsteps heralding the return of the last two guards. His partner and the engineer came ambling in to report their hitch had been as incident-free as the other shifts.

"Before we quit your energetic buddy took a look around from atop the mound," remarked Sanders.

"Nary a soul in sight, runt," drawled Stretch. "Sun rose about ten minutes ago — you can see for miles. And all I spotted was a jackrabbit or two."

"I guess it's no use tryin' to figure how soon the deputy's gonna show," said Larry.

"No use at all — anybody's guess," said Sanders. "Whatever needs doing at Fortuna Pass, hustling it would be too great a risk. Those volunteers have no choice but to work slowly."

"If the pass was wider, you'd've been out of here long before now," yawned Stretch.

"If it were wider, we wouldn't be here at all, there'd have been no need," said

Sanders. "Any driver could've skirted the pile-up." He shrugged fatalistically. "But, being narrow and high-walled — well — it's all been said."

The Fabers came in, followed by Kolbe, disgruntled at having cut himself while shaving with cold water, then Rossiter and the guard. The Texans and Sanders moved out to the well to work the windlass and raise the bucket to dash cold water into their faces. When they re-entered the bar-room, Chris was distributing laden plates, fish again.

Something was wrong.

Larry sensed it when they were half-way through the meal. No conversation, except for the few pleasantries exchanged by Sanders and the redhead. Why the prolonged silence, the tension in the air? At irregular intervals, Rossiter aimed scowls in his direction. The others had noticed, he realized, and were ill at ease.

When they had finished eating and were starting on their coffee, the preacher said gently, "We should give

144

thanks to the Lord this morning that no violence befell any of us last night."

"Amen," said his wife.

"I wonder if it might have been as peaceful a night, had we not decided to post guards," mused Sanders.

Rossiter now spoke up, and harshly. "All right, nobody got killed last night, but now we got somethin' else to fret about!"

"Sure have," growled Mallick.

The Fabers appeared apprehensive. Kolbe frowned at the stage driver and protested, "Surely not. Confound it, man, isn't a murderer in our midst trouble enough?"

"We got a thief here too," declared Rossiter.

"A thief?" challenged Sanders. "Why do you say that? What's missing?"

"My wallet." Rossiter was eyeing Larry again. "I wasn't totin' no fortune in it, but fifty-five dollars means a lot to a stage line man."

"Couldn't you have — just mislaid it?" asked Mrs Faber.

145

"Mislaid nothin'," retorted Rossiter. "Somebody lifted my wallet, lady, and it had to happen when Mister Kolbe and me were finishin' our shift — or a little while before."

Larry drained his cup, set it aside and remarked, "You keep cold-eyein' me, Rossiter. What's your gripe? You were back in your shack by the time I walked out of here." He glanced at Chris and recalled, "With you waitin' for me out front."

Kolbe snapped his fingers, his eyes gleaming maliciously.

"Something occurs to me," he said. "You could have woken long before you appeared, could have been outside when we were on guard."

"That's crazy," scoffed Chris.

"Downright ridiculous," protested Sanders. "Driver, you should guard your tongue. Rash accusations can only cause ill-feeling, and we can't afford . . . "

"I can't afford to be robbed," countered Rossiter.

146

Larry's hands were steady as he dug out his Durham-sack to build his first cigarette. Under other circumstances, Rossiter would have been bloody-nosed by now, flat on his back, out cold. He got to his feet, matching stares with the stage driver.

"You're accusin' me?" he drawled. Rossiter nodded grimly. "Dumb accusation. And you'd be payin' for it right now if things weren't this way, you havin' to drive the stage again when you get the word from San Raphael."

"Any fool calls us thieves, it costs him," muttered Stretch. "And then some."

"Please!" pleaded Faber. "No violence!"

"Fine by me — let's all cool down," said Larry. "Everybody listen up. My partner and me, we don't care cold beans about Rossiter's fifty-five dollars. Maybe we look like we're broke, but we ain't. Our bankroll tallies to around eight hundred right now. Kolbe's welcome to check it. And you,

Rossiter, you want to search me? Come on, check my pockets."

"This is terrible," fretted Mrs Faber.

"Madam, I remind you we know nothing of these men," Kolbe said sternly. "Nothing beyond what they've told us of themselves. And can we be sure that was the truth?"

"So let's *make* sure," growled Larry, eyeing Rossiter again. "C'mon, Big Mouth. Search me."

Mallick's jeering laugh started Texas blood boiling.

"Now ain't this a joke," sneered the guard. "As if you'd challenge Caleb to search you — with his wallet on you." To the other people, he opined, "He's stashed what he stole."

"Listen, you . . . !" began Stretch.

"Take it easy, amigo," soothed Larry. "We'll play this cool."

"How about we check your gear, saddlebum?" scowled Rossiter.

"You can do that," nodded Larry. "Check my partner's gear too if you want. One thing though. Don't call me saddlebum again, not if you value your front teeth."

"Lawrence, you don't have to hold still for this," frowned Sanders.

"Tell 'em to go to hell," urged Chris.

"Miss Brodie!" gasped Faber. "I beg you! Such *language*!"

"Their things *should* be searched," insisted Kolbe. "I've had my doubts about these roughnecks right from the start."

"Where's your stuff?" demanded Rossiter.

"Kitchen," Larry said curtly.

He and Stretch followed the crew, the other tagging along. Sizeable though it was, the kitchen became crowded. Rossiter bee-lined for Larry's saddlebags and, with his back turned, began rummaging. In a moment he was on his feet again, triumphantly exhibiting a wallet neither Texan had ever seen before.

"Here it is, by damn! My wallet!" He checked the contents. "With my cash still in it!"

149

"Guess you sneak-thieves ain't had a chance to divvy it up," jibed Mallick.

The Fabers expressed shock. Kolbe glowered accusingly while Sanders and the redhead traded dubious glances. Sceptical they were, but the doubt they shared was of the crew's actions, not of the drifters'.

"That wallet," Sanders said bitterly, "must have been planted in Lawrence's gear."

"You're being naive, sir," said Kolbe.

"I smell a set-up!" snapped Chris.

"Mister Lawrence — I don't know what to say," frowned Faber.

"You don't, huh?" growled Larry, his eyes travelling from face to face. "Well, *I* know what to say and I'm sayin' it. I didn't lift Rossiter's wallet and that goes for my partner too. Whatever you people think of us, we ain't thieves."

"Naturally you'd deny it," said Kolbe. "I believe you should leave and I'm sure I speak for the majority here. You don't have our trust, to put it mildly, and we'd all feel a great deal

150

more secure being rid of you."

"Speak for your fatheaded self, Big Shot!" flared Chris.

"Why don't we vote on it?" suggested Mallick.

"Lawrence said I'm in charge, and I say they ride," insisted Rossiter.

"What do *you* say, Mister Faber?" challenged Sanders. "And let's not forget charity, benefit of the doubt, judge not — and so on."

"In the face of the evidence . . . " Faber shrugged helplessly.

"So it gets down to that, huh preacher?" sneered Stretch.

"Groot's got the right idea, I reckon," said Rossiter, pocketing his wallet. "We vote to decide if they stay or go."

"I trust them, so I vote they stay," declared Sanders.

"Me too," Chris said defiantly.

But only those two supported the trouble-shooters. And now the tall men were impassive, matching stares with their accusers. Quietly, Larry told them, "Neither of us lifted no wallet, but we

151

can't force you to believe that, and we never stay where we ain't wanted."

"So we're gonna ride out of here?" asked Stretch.

"Right now," nodded Larry. "We'll head north — as far from Midas Mound as our horses'll take us."

"And good riddance," said Kolbe.

"Yeah," leered Mallick. "Get goin'."

And still Larry controlled his temper and, as always, Stretch followed his lead. While they collected and packed their gear, Sanders and the redhead stood close together, disassociating themselves from the main group, who followed the Texans' every movement as though suspecting they would take more than their own property.

Hefting rolled packs, filled saddlebags and sheathed Winchesters, they donned their Stetsons and made their exit by the rear door. Already, Larry had ideas about that rear door. It would have been all too easy for Rossiter to gain entry that way during his hitch at guard duty and secrete his wallet in a saddlebag. Or it might not have been done that way. The wallet could have been inside Rossiter's shirt. His back was turned to the watchers when he checked the saddlebag; no difficult chore, transferring the article, just a little sleight of hand would achieve this.

They were followed only by Sanders and Chris, as they trudged along to the livery stable. While they readied their mounts, Sanders spoke for both of them.

"We don't believe a word of it."

"Didn't reckon you would," shrugged Larry.

"But then you and Red got brains in your heads," muttered Stretch, "which them other travellers ain't."

"I still think it'll be some time before the pass is cleared," said Sanders. "Until then, we'll have to manage without you, but it won't be easy."

"You got gypped," complained Chris.

Larry glanced at her as he secured his cinches.

153

"Red, you and Sanders got to wait it out. We take it kindly, you talkin' up for us. But, when we're gone, don't make it rougher on yourself by wranglin' with the other passengers. That goes for you too, Sanders. Be a whole lot more comfortable for you both if you keep your ideas to yourselves."

"That has occurred to me," Sanders assured him. "Well, at least you know how *we* feel."

"Sure," grunted Stretch. "Muchas gracias."

Before mounting, they shook hands with Sanders. Unnoticed by the engineer, Larry flashed the redhead a quick look. She was intuitive and caught his meaning. A warning. She alone knew the travellers' temporary benefactors were more than they claimed to be, a couple of famous trouble-shooters in fact. In that one quick look, Larry had warned her to keep his and his partner's true identity a secret. She nodded to assure Larry she would do so, then came to them to stand on tiptoe and

154

kiss Larry's weatherbeaten cheek, then Stretch's.

They led their mounts out, swung astride and turned northward. For almost a mile they rode in silence. Larry glanced backward to satisfy himself they were well out of sight of Midas Mound, then turned eastward. Stirrup-to-stirrup with him, Stretch opined, "You never did figure on headin' way north."

"Not so you'd notice," growled Larry. "We're gonna ride a wide half-circle, make for the creek. We ain't through with them travellers yet."

During their swing toward the creek, Stretch aired his opinion of the significance of Rossiter's accusation and actions.

"We've learned somethin', huh? Still don't know which of 'em killed the tinhorn, but now we know the driver's a no-good liar, him and the guard both."

"Right," agreed Larry. "Don't prove either of 'em's the killer, but it's for sure they wanted us out of Midas

Mound — long gone and far away. They wanted that so bad, they set us up."

"Makes you plenty curious."

"You know it."

"So tell me if I'm readin' your mind, runt. We're gonna camp this side of the creek . . . "

"Right."

"Eatin' cold chow, on account of we ain't gonna have us a cookfire and show smoke that'll tip 'em we're still around."

"Right again."

"And we'll camp close by somethin' you can spy from with them field-glasses — tall tree or a hilltop."

"You read my mind good."

"Well . . . " The taller Texan shrugged and grinned a wry grin. "We've rid in each other's shadow a lot of years, ol' buddy, so I've had plenty practice."

"There's a rise, now that I recall," frowned Larry. "Not near our fishin' place. A mite west of it. Uh huh. A rise high enough. From atop it, we ought to be able to see far over the brush and get a clear sight of Midas Mound."

"Bueno," approved Stretch. "Let's find it."

They chose their position an hour later. Ideal for their purpose, ample concealment for their animals, good feed graze for them too, and the rise less than thirty yards from the creek-bank. While Stretch looked to the comfort of the horses, Larry broke out his field-glasses and hustled through the brush to the near base of the rise.

It took him only a few minutes to climb to the summit, and then he was belly-down, raising the glasses and bringing the abandoned mine camp into close focus. Stretch joined him a short time later.

"I was right," Larry told him. "We can see everything clear from here."

"What's happenin'?" asked Stretch, flopping beside him.

"No sign of movement," reported

Larry. "Can't see any of 'em."

"So they're stayin' out of the unfriendly hot sunlight," Stretch guessed. "Which'd be plumb uncomfortable for a gentle lady like the preacher's wife — and likely give Red a mess of freckles. All in the saloon I bet, talkin' about us. You suppose Red and the engineer-feller'll heed your advice? No wranglin' with the other folks?"

Larry lowered the binoculars and grimaced.

"I didn't make 'em swear they wouldn't," he said. "Sanders is his own man. And Red? You know how *she* is. Temper on a short fuse all the time. No, I could only deal out advice — couldn't ask 'em to promise."

"There's one thing irks me," Stretch confided. He took the glasses from his partner and studied the Midas Mound scene. "One thing I don't want to see happen, and you likely feel the same about it."

"What?" demanded Larry.

"That deputy from yonder of the

mountains," said Stretch. "Him that's gonna come tell 'em when the pass is cleared. After he shows up, they'll be on the move again muy pronto, all of 'em 'cept the tinhorn, him in the third grave in the cemetery. Nobody'll know who knifed him. They'll head on to San Raphael . . . "

"Report to the sheriff," nodded Larry. "He'll ask questions, but that's as much as he can do."

"They'll tell him about us," Stretch went on. "Maybe, when they describe us, talk of how tall we are, he'll guess it's us they're speakin' of. But, if he don't, he'll maybe figure it was one of us killed Arville and they shouldn't have let us get away. And how does *that* set with you?"

"Sticks in my craw," Larry said bitterly.

"Worst of it is — the real killer stays free," muttered Stretch. "That's why I don't want to see the deputy arrive. Longer it takes them toilers to clear a path through Fortuna Pass, longer the killer's stuck in Midas Mound — and maybe we'll get *some* chance of nailin' the sonofabitch."

"I got the same feelin', stringbean," declared Larry. "A two-bit tinhorn he was, that Arville. No friend of ours. We scarce got to know him. But some two-legged coyote put a knife in his heart and he *could* get away with it and the hell of it is nobody's gonna care. Arville'll be forgotten."

"By now, you got to be leery of *someone*," insisted Stretch. "Preachers ain't killers, their wives neither. You don't want to believe it was Sanders . . . "

"Take me a long time to forget what he did for me," breathed Larry, and his scalp crawled. "You saw."

"Sure enough," sighed Stretch. "Back there in the old shaft, I saw it all."

"Right atop where I was standin'." Larry's voice shook. "He caught on. I didn't. And, if he'd made his move a mite slower, just a mite slower, it wouldn't have been just me under the stuff fallin' in on us. He'd have got buried along with me."

"The redhead — we'll never believe she's the one," said Stretch. "No. Not Red. So that leaves just three. Rossiter and his buddy're a couple lyin' bastards, no question about that. But are we gonna rule the big shot out? How about this Kolbe?"

"You tell me," shrugged Larry, retrieving the field-glasses.

"Don't it strike you he brags too much?" challenged Stretch. "I mean, he wants everybody to know what an important hombre he is — like he's afeared they'll forget it. And would he be the first faker we ever ran into? Things ain't always like they seem, runt, and neither are folks."

"You maybe got a point," Larry agreed. "Meanwhile, there's somethin' irks *me* — plenty."

"What?" asked Stretch.

"We had to quit, didn't have no choice," grouched Larry. "So I'm here 'stead of snoopin' alongside the saloon, listenin' to what they're sayin'."

"Yeah," nodded Stretch. "I wish I could hear it too."

They were being discussed by the travellers, and the discussion was building up to a heated argument.

6

Gone But Not Forgotten

CHRIS was perched on the bar, her legs crossed, a riot of color in her bright green slippers, violet gown and a sizeable scarf of shrieking yellow with sky-blue polka dots. The Fabers sat at a table with Kolbe. Rossiter and Mallick had claimed the other table and Sanders, coatless so that his armpit-holstered handgun was well and truly visible, propping up the bar a few feet from where the redhead perched.

The argument was triggered by the engineer's first words, though he expressed himself quietly, unheatedly.

"I feel it's only fair everybody understands my attitude. I am not and will never be satisfied about the way Lawrence and his friend were made to leave."

163

"You're entitled to an attitude," Kolbe said pompously.

"It's all . . . " Faber shook his head sadly, "so unfortunate, so very unfortunate."

"This is a bad place," said his wife, shuddering. "I sense evil here."

"Well, Mrs Faber, it's natural you should feel that way," Sanders remarked. "Murder is evil, and it's certain murder was done here."

"I want to know why you feel so soft about them trail-tramps," muttered Mallick. "You ever meet 'em before?"

"Never," shrugged Sanders. "You could say I'm backing my instincts, that's all. I simply don't believe they're thieves."

"I don't believe it neither," declared Chris.

"Either," said Sanders.

"Okay — Teacher," she nodded. "Either."

"Before we expelled them, you warned us about rash accusations," Kolbe reminded Sanders. "*Now* who's

164

making rash accusations? Do you realize what you are saying to us, Sanders? I for one resent your inference!"

"His what?" frowned Rossiter.

"How's that again?" prodded Mallick.

"His inference, confound it!" fumed Kolbe.

"I beg you, Brother Kolbe, control your emotions," pleaded Faber. "This dissension is extremely distressing to my wife."

"My apologies, madam," Kolbe said through clenched teeth.

"Don't bother to beg *my* pardon, Big Shot," jibed Chris. "Just keep pretendin' like I ain't — am not here."

"I'll endeavor to make my point simply and as calmly as possible — under the circumstances," said Kolbe. "By his sceptism as to the obvious guilt of those roughneck cowhands, Sanders is inferring *one of us* picked the driver's pocket and, even worse, planted it in Lawrence's saddlebag."

Rossiter's eyes narrowed.

"That's what you think?" he growled at Sanders.

"If Lawrence and his friend are innocent, as I believe them to be, there's no other explanation," Sanders said, shrugging apologetically. "I'm sorry. I regret having to say it. Unfortunately, there's no diplomatic way of putting it."

"No use goin' off half-cocked," said Chris. "Thievery's small potatoes anyway when you stack it up against murder."

"As well as being a thief, Lawrence or his friend must've killed the gambler." Kolbe was suddenly shocked. "Thunderation! And we insisted they leave! An inexcusable error on our part. We should have disarmed them and held them for the deputy."

"Oh, my!" sighed Mrs Faber.

"Bull!" jeered Chris.

"Miss Brodie — really!" protested Faber.

"Bull!" Chris firmly repeated. "You jaspers ain't — aren't thinkin' straight.

Jerry was a stranger to the tall boys. Why'd one of them want to kill him? We know it wasn't robbery, so somebody tell me why? If you ask me, the killer . . . "

"Nobody asked you," chided Mallick.

"Button your lip — you're just hired help," retorted Chris. "And, like it or not, I'm gonna say it. The killer's still here, right here in this old saloon right now!"

All but Sanders eyed her askance; he frowned thoughtfully and lit a cigar. Kolbe flicked a speck of dust from his lapel and assured everybody, "The girl's too excitable for her own good. Personally, I am easier of mind now that those ruffians are far away from us. There's no doubt in my mind they are murderers and thieves and it offends me that they've made good their escape, but at least *we* are safe."

"Damn you," cried Chris. She dropped from the bar and advanced on him, eyes flashing. "What would *you* know? You ain't got the brains you were born with!"

She might have thrown herself at the Los Angeles man had Sanders not intercepted her. He was methodical as well as fast on his feet; he thought to set his cigar on the edge of the bar before heading her off. To restrain her, he had to gather her into his arms. She struggled but, to his great relief, did not claw at him nor kick his shins.

The driver and guard had tensed. The Fabers were alarmed and showing it. Kolbe was trembling.

"She's a harridan!" he gasped. "A wildcat!"

"And you're a stuff shirt and a damn blowhard jackass!" she raged.

Sanders still gripped her firmly.

"She'll calm down presently," he said. "Too bad this conference got out of hand. I'll take her outside. She could use some fresh air."

The redhead stopped struggling and allowed him to guide her to the batwings, out into the sunlight, then along to the shade thrown by a shack some distance away.

"All right, you can let go of me," she sighed. "I'll quit rantin' — now that I don't have to listen to that high and mighty Kolbe."

"As you wish," he said, releasing her. "But with regret. Yes, somewhat reluctantly."

"What're you talkin' about?" she demanded.

"You *were* a wildcat in there," he said with a faint grin. "I'll be ready to duck if what I'm about to say angers you. You felt good in my arms, Chris. Very real. Very appealing."

"Is that so?" she asked warily.

"Your clothes are far too gaudy, but there's a clean smell to you, not the scent of cheap perfume," he said. "Must be the soap you use. Or it could be just you? Do you mind my saying that? It's intended as a compliment, not a liberty."

"That's nice," she said. "I like how you talk, but maybe you ought to be

169

more particular. Careful who you take a shine to, Whit. You're educated and a gentleman and your work's important — and you know what I am."

"What you are," he nodded. "And what you *could* be."

"Wrong time, wrong place," she warned. "You better not forget it's us against them now." She gestured to the saloon. "We're the only two stood up for them drifters. They — aren't — forgettin' that, and one of 'em's a killer."

"Afraid?" he asked.

"Well," she said. "We could still be here tonight — when it'll be dark. The way I feel about that bunch, I wouldn't trust any of 'em. Don't you be surprised if I spend the whole night squattin' atop the mound wrapped in a blanket and not darin' to close my eyes."

"That sounds drastic — and uncomfortable for you," he said. "I think you trust me, so you'd feel safe bedding down in the saloon. I'd be there too in case something happens. Of course I'd insist you sleep in the kitchen and we'd prop a chairback against the knob of that back door, and I'd sleep in the bar room — but the preacher and his wife would be horrified, Kolbe in keen disapproval and, if Rossiter or the guard made any suggestive remarks, I'd have to fight them."

"You would?" she frowned.

He shrugged impatiently.

"It's expected. When a man is attracted to a woman, he assumes a certain responsibility, has to defend her good name."

"The driver and that Mallick slob're mean jaspers," she pointed out. "They'd likely beat hell out of you."

"I'd score a punch or two before I went down," he assured her.

"You'd do that?" She studied him intently. "For *me*?"

"I told you," he said. "It's expected. It's what a man's supposed to do."

"Better think it over, Whit," she advised. "Gettin' to like a girl so

171

different to you could be a real bad mistake."

"Or it could be a good thing," he said. "For both of us."

She showed him a rueful smile.

"As if we don't have enough on our minds, huh?"

"Yes," he agreed. "An avalanche, a stagecoach derouted, can have a lasting effect on travellers."

"I wonder if Jerry'd still be alive, if we hadn't come here," she mused. "What d'you think?"

"The question didn't occur to me before," he said, stroking his chin. "Was he murdered because we all found ourselves in Midas Mound? No, that couldn't be the reason. The killer had an opportunity here, no doubt about that, but I believe, if he hadn't been murdered here, it would have happened in San Raphael while we overnighted there, probably in his hotel room. Arville was marked for murder, Chris, and now I wonder if we'll ever learn why."

She turned to survey the mound.

"I got the right idea," she decided. "If we're still stuck here tonight, that's where I'll sit it out, right on top of that old mess of rock."

"Not by yourself," he said. "I'll be up there with you."

"You don't have to," she said.

"Yes," he insisted. "I do."

"You know, you aren't the first jasper wanted to be with me all night," she said moodily.

"They *wanted* — I *care*," he stressed. "There's a big difference, Chris, which I hope you appreciate."

★ ★ ★

Stretch had rolled on his back and catnapped a while with his Stetson shielding his face. Now he roused and glanced at Larry, still bellied down and scanning the camp through his field glasses.

"Any action, runt?"

"Not much," said Larry. "About a

173

quarter-hour ago, Red came out of the saloon with Sanders. They've been parleyin' private ever since."

"I guess, with us gone, they got plenty to fret about," remarked Stretch. "None of them others are their friends any more."

"That's why we'll keep on spyin' from here," Larry told him. "Somethin's gonna break sooner or later. And, when it does, they could need our help."

"Got a feelin' in your bones, huh?" prodded Stretch.

"Damn right," growled Larry.

"What kind of a somethin'?" asked Stretch.

"I wish I knew, wish I could guess," Larry said edgily. "This is the part that fazes me — not havin' any kind of notion."

"Leave them glasses," urged Stretch. "Mosey on back to the creek and rest your bones and your brains. I'll take over here. Anything special happens, I'll whistle you."

"Yeah, okay," nodded Larry.

He surrendered the binoculars, crawled back off the top of the hill and descended its south slope. Moving through the brush, he wracked his brain again. Was Kolbe what he claimed to be? Had he put that knife in the gambler, or had it been Rossiter or Mallick? His mood was grim by the time he sprawled on his back a little way from where the sorrel and pinto grazed, but then he acknowledged the futility of probing for answers. The hell with it. Better to resign himself to the prospect of awaiting developments. What option did he have?

* * *

Nine forty-five that morning, Deputy John Covington put his mount to the western ascent to Fortuna Pass. At intervals he veered clear of the trail to make way for wagons hauling rubble, big rigs minus canopies and heavily loaded, drawn by oxen. He traded nods with the drivers, but asked no questions. Why delay these men? He would save his questions for one Bartley Hayworth, the Sun Flats mine foreman in charge of the clearing operation.

Bulky Hayworth was taking a break, hunkered by a fire a few yards inside the west entrance to the pass, drinking coffee, when the deputy arrived. Reining up, Covington dismounted and stood arms akimbo a moment, studying the scene of activity. Another rig was being loaded. Volunteers sweated and strained to roll boulders from the pass floor and heave them into the wagon.

"Here to stay, Kid?" asked Hayworth, noting the sack of provisions slung to the deputy's saddle.

"Sheriff Lunceford's riders, Mister Hayworth," nodded Covington, hunkering beside him. "I'm to wait here and, soon as you give the word the stage can get through, ride to Midas Mound to tell the westbound's crew."

"Hope the hunting was good," said Hayworth. "Otherwise the folks at the Mound'll be plenty hungry."

"Great hunting thereabouts," grinned Covington. "Like I guaranteed 'em, they sure won't starve."

"Eastbound passengers're the lucky ones," remarked Hayworth. "They get to wait it out in a San Raphael hotel. Bet they're a whole lot more comfortable than the people off the westbound."

"How long do you figure, or is it too early for me to ask?" said the deputy, scanning the action again.

"Maybe before sundown," said Hayworth. "But, mind, I said maybe."

Covington's gaze fixed on a tarp-covered, square-shaped stack a respectful distance from this fire; its position was marked by a red flag.

"The dynamite," he said. "Will you be . . . ?"

"Won't be any blasting, and you can take that for a fact," declared Hayworth, raising his eyes to the high pass walls. "I ruled against it. Did some climbing since we got here, some climbing and checking. Setting off charges'd be more than our lives are worth. Can't take the chance in a place like this."

"Too much loose stuff up there?" prodded Covington.

"Too much," nodded Hayworth. "Sometimes, after a big rock-fall, what's left is solid. Sometimes it's not like that at all. Only *some* of the softened rubble comes down. And what's still up there could shake loose from the vibration of a gunshot — so what do you suppose'd happen if we tried blasting?"

"Holy Moses," breathed Covington.

"We're taking our lives in our hands — I hope the Hamilton Stage Line appreciates it — just moving all this rock out of the pass," said Hayworth. "Vibration, we can't avoid it, no way those rigs and teams can move smoothly."

"So all you can do is clear enough space for the coach to come through," guessed Covington.

"That's all," said Hayworth. "And

here's something you got to remember to tell the westbound's crew, because it's mighty important." He mouthed the warning emphatically. "After the east climb, the driver has to slow down. He doesn't hustle his team through here, understand? He lets the horses *walk*, he takes the coach through *slow* and *easy*. And the guard better not get careless with his shotgun, better be sure it's not cocked."

"I sure won't forget to tell 'em," Covington promised. "Uh — Mister Hayworth?"

"Yeah?"

"You think Fortuna Pass'll ever be safe again — I mean absolutely safe?"

"No, I don't, damn it. Didn't matter it being so narrow. Didn't matter before the storm. A lot of high country passes're narrow, but safe enough."

"But, whatever happened here . . . ?"

"Right. Whether it was lightning or the long hard rain, the damage has been done. I'll say that word again, young feller. Vibration. Still too much loose stuff way up there. Smartest move the Hamilton line could make would be to re-route, even if it means swinging clear around these mountains. Either that or hire surveyors who'll choose a section safe for blasting another opening, another way through."

The deputy rose and stared toward the east opening.

"Hey, they've cleared a fair strip already," he observed. "Maybe I'll be headed for Midas Mound a couple hours before sundown."

"You might be doing that," said Hayworth.

★ ★ ★

When Sanders and the redhead returned to the saloon, they were the centre of attention. Kolbe addressed the engineer officiously.

"May we hope you've convinced this young woman she should curb her temper?"

"Such an unseemly display of emotion," Mrs Faber murmured.

"Brothers and sisters, we should be charitable unto each other," begged Faber.

"Huh!" was Chris's scornful reaction to that plea.

Sanders moved to the bar to retrieve and relight his cigar, then turned to appraise his fellow-travellers.

"On the subject of Miss Brodie's temper, I have just this to say, and we'd all do well to heed it," he offered. "It's plain enough we're at cross-purposes, Miss Brodie and I believing Lawrence and Woodville to have been innocent of any wrongdoing, you people believing them to be both murderers and thieves. Isn't it also plain we'll achieve nothing by further argument? Can't we agree to hold to our own opinions, and without rancour?"

"Words of wisdom indeed, Brother Sanders," approved Faber. He appealed to the other men. "As intelligent human beings, surely we can . . . ?"

"Yeah, okay," shrugged Rossiter. "If Miss Hothead reins in her temper, I guess we can do likewise."

"Sweet reason must prevail," Mrs Faber said earnestly.

"Speakin' of reason," said Chris. "Seems reasonable to me you could help more'n you do — your ladyship. When it comes to keepin' us fed, I don't crave to be a solo act all the time."

"Dear Dora is not in the best of health, Sister Brodie," frowned Faber. "However, I'm sure she'll do her share as best she can."

"Somethin' else we'll have to think about," declared Chris.

"Like what, for instance?" challenged Mallick.

"Like *stayin'* fed, for instance," she retorted. "You should've thought of it before you voted for them tall boys to quit. They left some stuff for us, but not much, just a little coffee and fish enough for lunch. They'll hunt the next fresh meat they eat, and you and the driver better do likewise — else no supper tonight."

"If we're still in this pesthole tonight," scowled Kolbe.

"We have no guarantee we won't be," Sanders pointed out.

"Jackrabbit, if that's all you can shoot," said Chris, nodding to Mallick. "And any berries safe to eat. Shoot three — four'd be better — and I'll fix us enough stew to keep the cold out."

"We would be most obliged to you, Brother Mallick," said Faber.

"See what I can do," shrugged Mallick, making for the batwings.

After his partner had left, Rossiter grimaced and asked,

"Didn't happen to leave any booze behind, did they?"

"Alcohol has been the ruin of . . . " began Faber.

"They had liquor, some decent rye whiskey," said Sanders. "I'm sure they took it with them."

"How'd you know . . . ?" began Rossiter.

"On our first night here, when I shared this bar-room with them, they very kindly treated me," said Sanders. "We had just the one, a nightcap."

"You were quick, sir, to fraternize with them," frowned Kolbe.

"Trusted 'em at first sight, huh?" jeered Rossiter.

"I've never claimed to be an infallible judge of character but, yes, I trusted them at first sight," nodded Sanders. He aimed a bland grin at the Fabers. "Do not recoil in horror. It wasn't exactly a drunken orgy. We had, as I said, just the one."

"How very fortunate for you," commented Kolbe. "Well, as you seemed clear-headed enough the following morning, we'll take your word for it."

"Not every drinkin' man I've known was a stumble-drunk." Chris assured everybody. "Drinkin' men, there's all kinds. Some know their limit and some don't know when to cork the bottle."

"Nevertheless, hard liquor has been

the downfall of many," intoned Faber.

"I remember I proposed a toast," Sanders reminisced. "Let me see if I can recall the sentiments I expressed . . . "

"Don't bother," said Kolbe.

"I don't believe we want to hear," said Faber.

"Oh, you should, you really should," insisted Sanders. "How could you disapprove of such a toast? And I think, yes, I recall it now."

"How'd it go?" asked Chris. "I'd like to hear, even if nobody else does."

"I began, of course, with my hosts, wishing them luck," said Sanders. "Then it went like this, May Miss Brodie find happiness somewhere, may Mathew Faber be granted many years of fruitful ministry, may Jerry Arville be dealt a pat hand, may Horace Kolbe continue to prosper and may our driver and guard never be menaced by bandits."

"Didn't wish anything for yourself?" asked Chris. Sanders grinned as he remembered.

"Lawrence was as thoughtful as you. He reminded me I'd overlooked myself."

"Most gentlemanly of him," Kolbe said scathingly.

"And just what'd *you* wish for?" challenged Rossiter.

"Just the hope that the employees of the mining company I'm to work for will patiently await my late arrival," said Sanders. "I'm to plan and supervise the drilling of shafts, you see, and that's a job best handled by a specialist."

"Wasn't no specialists bored that shaft you near got buried inside of, huh?" grinned Rossiter.

"No." The engineer's face clouded over. "Insufficient shoring. Ceiling beams about to give way. They probably made the potentially fatal error of trying to economize on lumber."

"Must you remind us?" complained Kolbe, mopping his brow. "I have a horror of — such calamities — just the thought of being buried alive . . ."

"If the idea spooks you, don't talk of

it, forget it," advised Chris. She turned to Sanders. "You too. It was rough while it lasted, but now it's over and you ought to put it out of your mind — else you could have nightmares."

"I trust you gave thanks for your deliverance, Brother Sanders," said Faber.

"You can bet your Bible I did," Sanders fervently assured him.

"I never bet," said Faber.

"Sorry," said Sanders.

Kolbe became restless. He rose and paced.

"This delay — worst thing that could happen to me," he declared. "Some inconvenience to you people, but a far greater inconvenience to me. Your job will be waiting, Sanders, when you reach — I've forgotten your destination . . . "

"Vargas," said Sanders. "Arizona Territory."

"And no doubt you'll . . . " Kolbe paused to look at Faber, "carry on with your ministry or whatever you call it. But it's more difficult for me. I am president and general manager of all Kolbe enterprises, all of them, the stores, the real estate interests, every facet of our business operations. I delegate authority to certain reliable members of my vast staff, but the big decisions rest with me. I do all the planning, the executive administration, the distribution of cash assets to profit-making speculations."

"A heavy burden I'm sure," Faber sympathized.

"I'm equal to it," bragged Kolbe. "But I need to be there. I should be well on my way to Los Angeles by now, not pinned down in a played-out mining camp by a freak of Nature."

"An act of God, Brother Kolbe," insisted Faber.

"Amen," nodded his wife.

"Sounds like big business," remarked Rossiter.

"One of the biggest in California, hardly a two-bit concern," Kolbe said irascibly.

"I guess you'd have to be one of the richest passengers ever bought passage on a Hamilton stage," said Rossiter.

"That's entirely possible," nodded Kolbe. He resumed his chair and drummed the edge of the table with pudgy fingers. "I should *never* leave Los Angeles, and wouldn't have, but for responsibilities of another kind — family responsibilities. My brother Adam chose a fine time to fall ill, I don't think. And, of course, he'd have to be living in a place like Tulsa, hundreds of miles from Los Angeles."

"It was your *duty*, Brother Kolbe," Faber said warmly. "And I will pray for his rapid recovery."

"Nothing critical I hope?" asked Sanders.

"Some kind of kidney ailment," shrugged Kolbe. "He's over the worst of it. But that sister-in-law of mine becomes panic-stricken and exaggerates everything. The way she composed the telegram, Adam might've been at Death's door — fool of a woman."

"Any kidney problems can be painful — extremely painful," Sanders pointed out.

"An unnecessary journey — and a long one," scowled Kolbe. "Board meetings postponed at my head office, several negotiations half-completed . . . " He seethed with impatience. "My prolonged absence will cause *chaos*. I'll be returning to an absolute *shambles*!"

"I just decided somethin'," Chris remarked to Sanders.

"Yes?" he asked.

"Yeah," she nodded. "After hearin' old Money-Bags blowin' off steam and frettin' like crazy, I've made up my mind I'll never try to be boss of a big business. Not worth the hassles. Better to be poor and happy than rich and miserable."

"That's a facetious remark," chided Kolbe.

"Her with her smart mouth," growled Rossiter.

"A little levity — where's the harm?" Sanders appealed to them. "We've had more tension than we anticipated here in Midas Mound, little to smile about and, really, a touch of humour should be welcomed rather than criticized."

"That's *your* opinion," snapped Kolbe.

"Yes," said Sanders. "For what it's worth."

"Well, I don't appreciate it," Kolbe said sourly.

"A pity," remarked Sanders. "The last important businessman I knew had the same attitude, all business, no sense of humour, fretting all the time, and what did it win him? He suffered a seizure and never recovered, died at a too-early age. Forty-one I believe. Something to think about, Kolbe."

"I *thrive* on the responsibilities of decision-making, thank you," said Kolbe's curt retort. "And I enjoy excellent health."

"Glad to hear it," said Sanders.

From the northeast, they heard the echo of a rifle shot, then another.

"Fish for lunch, rabbit stew for supper," said Chris. "Now don't that beat goin' hungry?"

"The Lord provides," Faber said piously.

An hour later, the four riders advancing from the west reined up to spell eight horses. McGrail, Arno, Elkin and Rolfe had emerged from a stand of timber and, from where they now sat their mounts, scanned the expanse of brushy terrain ahead. A faint breeze blew from the east offering some relief from the heat.

McGrail rose in his stirrups, nudged his Stetson off his brow and stared a while.

"See somethin'?" demanded Rolfe.

"A ways off, but I don't reckon my eyes're playin' tricks," said McGrail. "Smoke."

"Could be Midas Mound?" suggested Arno.

"Uh huh, smoke from a chimney maybe," nodded McGrail. "We could be gettin' close."

After the horses had rested, they pressed on, and soon the spiral of smoke was clearly visible and a familiar aroma wafting their way.

"Somebody's fryin' fish," opined Elkin.

"All right now, let's remember what we decided," urged Arno. "After we say our say, it'll be up to Blystone. He's the boss."

A short time later, his partner's soft but audible whistle brought Larry to his feet.

7

In Desperation

AT the sound of Larry approaching through the brush, Stretch lowered the glasses a moment, turned and beckoned. The gesture spoke volumes; Larry should climb the hill fast to see what the taller Texan had seen.

He made the ascent in leaps and bounds and reached the summit panting. Dropping, he crawled forward to join his partner.

"Somethin'?"

"Sure enough. Horses headin' in from the west, eight of 'em, but only four riders."

Stretch surrendered the binoculars. Larry propped his elbows and focussed on the intermittently visible shapes traversing the area west of the ghost town.

"Yeah, you read it right. The four spares're wearin' saddles."

"What d'you make of 'em?" frowned Stretch.

"Beats the hell out of me," muttered Larry. "Party from San Raphael fetchin' supplies? Maybe, but I wouldn't bet on it. The next hombre them travellers expect'll be the deputy comin' to tell 'em they can move out. I don't know about this bunch."

"So we wait and see," guessed Stretch. "And that'll irk you plenty. You got no patience, runt."

"Well, I'd give my eye-teeth to know if they're friendlies or hostiles," grouched Larry.

"If they're bandidos . . . " began Stretch.

"That's the hell of it," said Larry. "Maybe Sanders is good with that pistol of his, but it'd be him and the crew against four. Kolbe and the preacher'd be no help."

Mallick had returned some time before with a catch of five jackrabbits.

As he entered the saloon, he and the other people heard the hoofbeats. He traded glances with Rossiter. The redhead came out of the kitchen to frown at Sanders. Kolbe rose eagerly, exclaiming, "And about time too! At last the deputy! The pass has been cleared and we can resume our journey!"

"We're hearing more than one horse, Kolbe" said Sanders.

"Maybe a posse?" suggested Chris.

"Might's well go out and see for ourselves," decided Rossiter, starting for the batwings.

Mallick and the Los Angeles man hurried after him. The Fabers followed, Sanders and Chris bringing up the rear. They grouped in front of the saloon and, moments later, the riders leading the saddled horses came into view around the north end of the mound.

Of the travellers, the only one suddenly feeling disquiet was the redhead, and she didn't know why; it was just an instinctive reaction to the sight of four blandly-grinning, well-armed strangers.

"Howdy there." Arno nodded a greeting as they drew rein. "You'll be the folks got stuck here on account of the pile-up at Fortuna Pass, right?"

"And we've been here far too long for my convenience," declared Kolbe. "Have you come to tell us we may leave now?"

"Not in that coach, mister," drawled Arno. "We heard in San Raphael there's just no guessin' how soon them rock-haulers'll finish their chore. Big chore, you know?"

"On the other hand . . ." McGrail dismounted and his cronies followed suit. "Any of you folks wantin' to get out of here in a hurry, why, we'll be glad to escort you to San Raphael. That's why we fetched four extra saddle-animals along."

"But we can only take four," said Elkin.

The horses were tied in front of the saloon and buildings either side of it.

Rossiter and Mallick were smoking, seeming only casually interested in the newcomers, who were now addressed by Faber, commending them for their concern for the plight of stranded travellers. Sanders was merely curious until he glanced at Chris and noted her expression; he tended to be respectful of women's intuition.

From their vantagepoint to the south, the Texans watched and waited.

"How's it look now?" asked Stretch.

"Parley," said Larry, holding the people in close focus. "And I wish I could hear what they're sayin'."

"You can't have everything," said Stretch.

"It is imperative I resume my journey without further delay," declared Kolbe. "Gentlemen, I for one accept your kind offer."

"Brother Kolbe, I fear you would suffer great discomfort travelling horseback," protested Faber.

"I loathe riding, but my time is valuable — haven't I made that clear?"

198

Kolbe ignored Faber and assured the strangers. "It will take me only a few minutes to pack my valise."

"Fine," said Rolfe. "We don't mind waitin'."

"No hurry," drawled McGrail. "How about you and your lady, Reverend?"

"And you folks?" Arno eyed Sanders and the redhead enquiringly. "You could double up if you want."

Sanders was undecided, but then Chris said firmly, "No thanks. I'd as soon wait till the stage can roll again."

"You?" prodded Arno.

"I think I'll wait it out," said Sanders.

"You people may suit yourselves," shrugged Kolbe. "This is an opportunity I can't afford to miss. Who knows how long it will take those workmen at the pass to . . . ?"

"The rough journey to San Raphael by horseback . . ." began Faber.

"Confound it, man, I make my own decisions!" snapped Kolbe.

"I can't dissuade you?" Faber asked pleadingly.

"My mind is made up," insisted Kolbe.

"Too bad," said Faber. "You've forced my hand — rich man."

Kolbe almost fainted. Sanders was shocked to the core by the swift transformation. It all happened in a matter of seconds. Faber was no longer stoop-shouldered when he swept his coattails back and, from the rear of his pants, produced a .45. Rossiter and Mallick promptly drew and levelled their pistols, as did the four newcomers.

Stretch felt his partner tense.

"What . . . ?"

"Big change!" breathed Larry. "All of a sudden they filled their hands, not just the four that just rode in — the preacher and the crew too!"

"Holy Hannah!" gasped Stretch.

"Take a look," urged Larry, proffering the binoculars. "I still can't figure this deal — but it's like no hombre's what he's supposed to be."

Chris had edged closer to the stunned Sanders. Now he was noting the change in the other woman. The 'preacher's wife' was smirking at the grinning McGrail and Arno, and the other strangers trading greeting with Rossiter and Mallick.

"What d'you say, Caleb?"

"Howdy, Groot."

Rossiter and Mallick acknowledged these greetings, then glanced at the man known to the passengers as Mathew Faber, who appraised the new arrivals and said knowingly, "Safe guess why you four showed up here. Worrying about your cut, Philo?"

"Hell, you know better'n that, Jarv — ," frowned Rolfe. "It ain't like that at all. We just figured you and Verna'd crave to get out of here."

"I — d-don't understand . . . !" faltered Kolbe. "What is the meaning of . . . ?"

"I said you forced my hand," said the man called Jarv. "You with your

201

bragging of your wealth and position. You're an idiot, Kolbe. A man of your importance should be more discreet." The voice was different, Sanders was reflecting. Nothing but his clothing remained of Preacher Mathew Faber. He guessed the name he answered to, Jarv, was short for Jarvis. Who *was* this man? He was still talking, jeering at the bug-eyed Kolbe. "I couldn't let you leave with four of my men. You'll be leaving, make no mistake about that, but with all of us."

"Life's full of surprises, huh Money-Bags?" taunted Verna.

To McGrail and his companions, the bogus preacher explained, "The big-mouth is Horace Kolbe, rich, important, a man of affairs. Compared to the ransom we'll demand, the loot in my valise is chicken-feed."

"Blystone, we took seventy-five thousand from that Quimera bank, so let's not call it chicken-feed," grinned Rossiter.

"Before I forget." Jarvis Blystone

drew a bead on Sanders. "That one packs a shoulder-holstered iron. Disarm him, one of you, and do it carefully, get behind him. Sanders, do I have to tell you what to do with your hands?"

Grim-faced, Sanders raised his hands.

"The Brodie bitch claimed she's heeled," Verna reminded Blystone.

"Want to search her?" grinned Blystone. "Give the boys a treat?"

As the woman started for her, Chris spoke sharply.

"Keep your distance. You can have my pistol — but I don't want you pawin' me."

Rossiter and the other hard cases loosed whistles as the redhead raised the skirts of her bright violet gown to reveal shapely legs and a garter-holstered derringer. She flushed, drew the tiny weapon and tossed it away.

Kolbe found his voice again.

"This is monstrous!" he blustered, as McGrail got behind Sanders and took possession of his Smith & Wesson.

"Why don't you just shut up."

growled Blystone.

"Hey, wasn't there six of you on that stage?" asked Elkin, glancing around.

"At the start, yes," nodded Blystone. "Of all the crazy luck. A tinhorn name of Arville. He was in the Keller Territorial Prison same time as I was. That was many a year ago. I wore my hair long then, had a thick beard too . . . "

"You're handsomer without whiskers, Jarv honey," smiled Verna.

"*You* did time?" growled Mallick. "Damn it, you can sure keep a secret!"

"You claimed you could only use smart hombres with no record back when you organised this outfit," frowned Arno.

"Now you tell us you're the only one of us ever saw the insides of a prison?" challenged Rolfe.

"Don't get hot about it," said Blystone. "I've never been recognized and never will be, because I'm a smart actor when I have to be. But Arville was a possible danger. I caught him sizing me up during the run from Quimera. Plain enough he was trying to put a name to me, maybe even wondering how I'd look long-haired and bearded. I just couldn't take a chance."

"So it was you knifed poor Jerry," sneered Chris.

"No," grinned Blystone. "I had Groot take care of him."

"You told me what to do, but you never did tell me why it had to be done," Mallick said resentfully.

"Faber — Blystone — or whatever your name is, you're the lowest breed of hypocrite," Sanders said bitterly. "It makes me sick to my stomach, remembering your burial service for a man butchered at your command, all the fake piety, the psalm-singing."

"Like I said, I'm a smart actor when I need to be," drawled Blystone.

"Quite an organizer too, it would seem," observed Sanders. "What happened to the driver and guard replaced by your own men? I suppose their bodies will never be found."

"Nothing so clumsy, Mister Engineer, nothing so obvious," said Blystone. "I had Caleb and Groot sign on as regular crew of the Hamilton Line six months ago. They've been working the east-west run all that time, two aces up my sleeve to be called into action when required. All my men are specialists of one kind or another. You're right and I thank you for the compliment. I *am* quite an organizer — a brilliant organizer."

"Modest too," jibed Chris.

"Kolbe, you should feel honored," declared Blystone. "You are now a prisoner of the No Name Gang."

"Yeah, we're famous," chuckled McGrail.

"We've had the law runnin' round in circles," bragged Elkin. "They don't know who we are or where we'll hit next."

"You'll eat regular and enjoy some degree of comfort during your stay with us," Blystone assured Kolbe. "Believe me, it's my intention to release you unharmed, provided of course the great corporation you founded comes across with the ransom money."

"How much're we gonna make 'em pay, Jarv?" asked Rossiter.

"A fortune, compared with the seventy-five thousand you boys are so eager to share," said Blystone. "The figure I have in mind is two hundred thousand."

"No!" groaned Kolbe. He was haggard now, his complexion ashen. "They won't pay — I'm not worth fifty dollars as a hostage — let along two hundred thousand! Please — don't kidnap me!"

"Hell, he's gonna bust out weepin'," sneered Arno.

"He's disgusting," Verna said disdainfully.

"I mean it!" gasped Kolbe. "You have to believe me!"

"Believe what?" challenged Blystone. "Go on, rich man, make your pitch. It'll probably be amusing, and I enjoy a good laugh."

"I'm *not* Horace Kolbe!" wailed the Los Angeles man. "I only pretended to be! My real name is Wilbur Wilkie and — I'm just a file clerk at Kolbe Enterprises. It's true I was granted leave to visit my sick brother in Tulsa — but that's the *only* truth of — everything I've said of myself. I lied. Horace Kolbe is safe in Los Angeles — probably taking lunch at Delgardo's or the Hotel de Vries — places I couldn't afford — even a sandwich or a cup of coffee."

"Are you gonna fall for that hogwash, Jarv?" growled Arno.

"I'm not lying now!" cried Kolbe. He shuddered and, looking at him now, Sanders felt his scalp crawl. The man was broken, a shabby caricature of what he had claimed to be, still pleading — and on his knees. "I implore you — don't hurt me — don't kidnap me! Oh, Lord, I wish I'd never pretended . . . "

"You believe him?" frowned Verna.

Blystone grimaced in contempt.

"Yes, I believe the fat bastard," he nodded. "Look at him, grovelling there. He's nothing — and worth nothing to us. He has to be an insignificant clerk. This is no act, Verna. He just isn't a good enough actor to fool me."

"Had us *all* fooled," said Mallick. "Includin' you."

"But not any more," said Blystone. "Griff, you and Philo stand guard over the three of them. Verna, the boys'll be hungry, so you start dishing up. Caleb, go check the area northwest for dust. I think it's too early for that deputy to show, but we'll take no chances. As soon as we eat, we're pulling out."

"And just what are your plans for us?" Sanders grimly demanded.

"I ain't waitin' to find out!" gasped Chris.

With that, she turned and took to her heels, running south for the brush. Blystone grimaced irritably. Rolfe levelled his Colt.

"No," chided Blystone. "If the deputy *is* on his way, a shot would alert him. One of you go after her."

"Hey, *I'm* volunteerin' for *that* chore!" leered Mallick. "Got plans for that redhead." As he moved to one of the spare horses, he added, "Don't wait lunch for me, boys. I'll bring her back — but not till I'm through with her, if you get what I mean."

"Don't try to be a hero," McGrail warned the suddenly agitated Sanders, drawing a bead on his belly.

Atop the rise to the south, Larry cursed in frustration.

"We got to do *somethin'*!" pleaded Stretch.

"You think I don't *want* to?" raged Larry.

"I didn't mean . . . " began Stretch.

"You see as clear as me," scowled Larry. "So you *know* we're hamstrung! We could pick him off from here, the sonofabitch chasin' Red. Sure, we could save *her*, but what of the *other two*? They hear a shot, they got Sanders and Kolbe for shields — and I owe Sanders."

"We can't even head that rider off and clobber him quiet," Stretch now realized. "They'll be expectin' him back at the Mound and, when he don't show . . ."

"Head back to our horses and saddle 'em," urged Larry. "Yours first, in case you can grab Red and hide her from him. That's the only idea I can come up with right now. Hustle!"

"'Be seein' you," said Stretch.

He made the descent fast and bounded away through the brush. The redhead, meanwhile, was also heading for the creek, but some distance west. And only by chance was she destined to reach it ahead of her pursuer. Mallick swore obscenely as his mount began struggling; his rein had caught in eight foot high brush and become entangled. As he fumbled to extricate it, Chris emerged from the growth and came to a halt panting.

She had reached ten feet of open ground between the brush and the creek-bank, thirty feet above the water at this section. Staring down, she wondered about the depth of the stream. Her gaze fixed on a half-submerged rock some distance from the opposite bank. Could she conceal herself behind it — assuming she could reach it?

"What the hell choice have you got?" she challenged, as she began unfastening her gown. "Just be thankful somebody threw you in a pond when you were in pigtails. At least you can swim. Didn't you learn the hard way?"

She removed gown and petticoat and, with a flash of inspiration, knotted two corners of the bright yellow scarf to the neck of the gown. Hearing threshing and stamping in the brush to her rear, she calculated she might just have time enough to fool the man hunting her.

At the outer edge of the drop, poised in nought but her most intimate underwear, she swung her clothing and let go. The gown, with petticoats and scarf adhering, sailed through the air and fluttered down, down, down, falling midstream. Then she dived, filling her lungs as she hurtled toward the water, the location of the rock memorized.

She went in cleanly and her luck was holding. At this point, the water was deep enough; she would not fracture her skull nor break her neck on the creekbed.

His horse able to move again, Mallick followed his quarry's path southward through the brush and reached open ground. At once, he noted the footprints leading to the outer edge. The horse was already difficult to handle, its right shoulder and left flank scratched by brush, so he dismounted, ground-reined it and stepped to the edge to scan the waterway.

A flash of familiar color caught his eye. The gown with the yellow scarf attached was being carried downstream and, from this distance, he couldn't detect the difference. He assumed what he glimpsed to be the body of his intended victim, who had now reached the far side of the half-submerged rock by swimming under water.

She broke the surface, pressing herself against the rock's far side, wheezing, catching her breath.

"Careful," she warned herself. "Hair as bright red as yours — you can see it for miles. Wait a minute, it's wet, so it's darker, so may be he won't spot you — and you got to know, damn it!"

Treading water, she swept her saturated hair to the back of her head and edged half of her face around the rock to stare upward. The figure opposite was briefly visible, Mallick, standing arms akimbo, staring downstream.

"That's it, you lousy skunk, that's me you see, poor drowned dead me. *Believe* it, you bum."

Plainly, Mallick was convinced; her ruse had worked. She saw him shrug, turn his back, move to his horse and remount. Then he disappeared into the brush and she loosed a sigh of relief.

No shivering. The water was cool, but the day uncomfortably warm. What to do now? She was safe for the moment though, thanks to her penchant for flimsy underwear, near naked. A century ahead of her time in some respects was Chris Brodie. Let other women suffer the discomfort of corsets, camisoles and knee-length drawers in century temperatures. Not for her, not so anybody would notice. Under the gown and petticoats, nought but the minimum essentials.

She was gradually getting it all together, recovering from the shock exposures triggered by the arrival of four desperadoes with four spare horses. So the preacher was no preacher, a boss-outlaw no less. And, spitefully, Chris doubted that Verna, alias Dora, was Mrs Blystone. More likely Blystone's paramour. And old Money-Bags wasn't what he had claimed to be. Hell, what a pitiful slob.

"But you should complain? You got away. What about Whit? What's gonna happen to that sweet gentleman, him that says he cares?"

It seemed far-fetched, but now she was thinking about it, wondering if she could sneak back to Midas Mound and — somehow — rescue Whit Sanders. Crazy? Maybe not. The No Name Gang would forget her after that polecat Mallick returned to report she had drowned. But what could she actually *do*? Inspiration failed her. Well, first things first. She wasn't helping anybody cringing behind this rock.

This time, she didn't have to swim underwater.

The Texans, meanwhile, were plagued by uncertainty. All Stretch could do was mount his pinto and move cautiously along the creek-bank and wonder what had become of the redhead. All Larry could do was watch from atop the rise, watch Mallick ride out of the brush and head back to Midas Mound — and

216

wonder what had become of the redhead.

"If you ran her down and killed her, Mallick," he was thinking, "I'll make you pay — in blood."

Sanders and the quivering Los Angeles man had been forced to squat together in the harsh sunlight between the mound and the saloon. Griff Arno and Philo Rolfe hunkered in shade, covering them with cocked six-guns. Inside, Blystone and the others partook of the food dished up by his mistress.

"Why, Wilkie?" The engineer nudged the pudgy man, and none too gently. "Come on, tell me. I'm trying to understand why you masqueraded as Horace Kolbe. What was the point?"

"You *couldn't* understand," mumbled Wilkie. "How could you, a qualified engineer, a professional, know how it feels to be a nonentity? Nobody paid any attention to me — all the years I worked for the corporation. I was almost an invisible man, a humble file clerk hidden away in a basement, the records section of a vast business empire, a lonely bachelor of no account."

"A wise man is content with his lot, takes pride in his work, no matter how lowly it may be," chided Sanders.

"I wanted to be noticed — I wanted identity — respect."

"You couldn't think of a better way, something better than playing at being a distinguished businessman?"

Wilkie bowed his head and sighed heavily.

"I succumbed to the temptation when — I was buying my return passage in Tulsa. Wearing my best clothes, I thought — how wonderful it could be, how it would feel to — command respect — be regarded as a man of importance. So, yes, I gave my name as Horace Kolbe and, for once in my humdrum life, asserted myself. Oh, glory! Such a marvellous feeling!"

"Was it worth it?" challenged Sanders.

"For a while, yes," said Wilkie, nodding wearily.

"Pretension is pathetic," scowled Sanders.

He looked up, sweat streaming into his eyes. The lone rider was moving in from the south, taking his time. What of Chris? he wondered, studying Mallick's face.

"Didn't look to see you so soon, Groot," grinned Arno. "She give you the slip?"

"Hell, no," Mallick growled as he reined up. "Damn fool bitch drowned herself." He dismounted and, while tying the horses, noted Sanders's grim gaze. "You don't like that, huh? Disappointed? Maybe *you* had plans for her?"

"You bastard!" gasped Sanders.

Mallick chuckled, strode to him, bent and gave him the back of his hand. The blow stung, but Sanders was immune to physical pain now. The mental anguish was something else. Anguish? Yes, why delude himself? That ill-fated young woman, so hard-boiled, so fiercely independent, but so

219

vulnerable. Lord, how he had craved to protect her, to make her smile, to hear her laugh, to offer her security and happiness. He *could* have made her happy — as his wife — and now she was lost to him.

"Sure, Groot?" Rolfe asked.

"Sure, I'm sure," drawled Mallick, about to enter the saloon. "Saw the body driftin' downstream."

"She cooked a fine mess of fish," remarked Arno. "We've ate. Better get in there, Groot, and get your share. We'll be movin' out soon as Jarv decides what we're gonna do to these jaspers."

Atop the rise, Larry lowered his glasses. The scene was imprinted in his mind, Mallicks reappearance at Midas Mound, Sanders and the Los Angeles man helpless prisoners under guard of two gunmen. And Mallick had returned alone. What had become of the redhead? Inactivity frayed his nerves. He slung the binoculars to his shoulder, edged back and began descending the south slope.

Stretch was, at his moment, reining up and gawking incredulously. What in tarnation was *that* — rising from the shallows dead ahead? Quite an apparition, a startling sight to see, was Chris Brodie, spotting him, wading out and moving toward him, hair streaming, body glistening, underwear clinging. To his deep relief, she moved easily, so it was clear she had suffered no injury. And now it was her turn to wax incredulous.

"It's *you* — *Stretch*!" she cried. "Well, if you ain't a sight for sore eyes, and me thinkin' I'd never see you or Larry again!"

"We — uh — only pretended to quit," he frowned. "Doubled on back here to keep an eye on — 'scuse me." He swung down and began unfastening his packroll. "Got to get you covered decent."

"Wait till you hear what . . . !"

"Sure, Red. We know some of it, been spyin' on the Mound through

221

field-glasses. I know you got plenty to tell us and Larry'll want to hear it, but first . . . "

"What's that?"

"My other shirt. Well, doggone it, we got to put *somethin'* on you — can't leave you near bare as the day you got born!"

"On me, it'll look like a tent, but what the hell? Let me have it."

When she had donned and buttoned the garment, it hung loose on her all the way down to her feet. He rescued his packroll, got mounted and offered his hand. She grasped it and swung up behind him, and then he was wheeling the pinto and starting back along the bank.

Until they came into view, Larry was pacing beside his sorrel, slamming his right fist into his left palm. He froze, staring hard, as the redhead waved to him. They arrived and he moved to the pinto to help her down and the anger in his eyes chilled her blood. His voice was harsh when he demanded to be told what Mallick had done to her.

"Simmer down, Big Boy." She winced to the grasp of his hands on her shoulders. "Whatever plans that skunk had for me, I didn't give him a chance. Look, there's a lot I got to tell you." She disengaged herself from his grasp and seated herself on his dumped gear. "But I'm still shook up and — dry in my throat now. Buy a lady a drink, fellers?"

Stretch made short work of breaking out a bottle and tin cup and half-filling it. She sipped eagerly and color returned to her cheeks. Larry, his compassion aroused, hunkered beside her and fished out his makings; Stretch followed suit.

"Take your time, Red." Larry spoke gently now. "You're safe with us."

"No, I got to tell it fast!" she insisted. "*I'm* safe now, sure, but *he* ain't!"

"Meanin' Sanders," he said.

"And Wilkie," she nodded.

"Who's Wilkie?" demanded Stretch.

"Old Money-Bags ain't Kolbe — he's Wilkie." She drained the cup and returned it to Stretch. "And the preacher ain't a preacher. Hell, nobody but Whit and me're what we're supposed to be. It's all mixed up and, listen, I'll start from when them hard cases showed up and tell it all, but you got to listen careful because there ain't time for me to say it twice."

Larry's cigarette was half-smoked when she paused to catch her breath. It had spilled out of her in jerky sentences, every detail of everything that had occurred since the bogus preacher revealed himself for what he was, a boss-outlaw, leader of a band of desperadoes known as the No Name Gang.

"How about this, runt?" Stretch's expression was as grim as his partner's. "Only way she could shake off that sonofabitch was make him believe she drowned herself."

"She *could've* drowned," scowled Larry.

"Not me," she retorted. "I swim like a fish."

"I guess," said Stretch, "We're gonna . . ."

"You bet your double-cinched saddle we're gonna," nodded Larry. "I owe Sanders."

"Best go in on our own feet, huh?" suggested Stretch, unfastening his spurs. "Ridin' in, they'd hear us before we got close enough to help Sanders or the other jasper."

"That's how we'll have to do it," muttered Larry. "So the stage crew're part of the gang? Some cunnin' coyote, this Blystone. All right, Blystone, Rossiter and Mallick and the four that fetched the spare horses makes seven."

"That ain't too many for us," shrugged Stretch.

"Never was before, won't be this time," said Larry.

"You better not forget Blystone's woman," warned Chris, and her face contorted. "That lousy, cheatin'

225

trash — makin' with the sweet talk and the oh-so-holy manners like butter wouldn't melt in her mouth. Damn her! To find my pistol, she was ready to strip me for all them skunks to gawk at! When I get my hands on her . . . !"

"Forget it," said Larry. "You're stayin' right here where you'll be safe."

"You already did enough, did your duty good, Red," Stretch said admiringly. "Wasn't for you, we'd be stuck again, no way we could move on 'em. We couldn't shoot Mallick off of his horse without tippin' our hand, you see."

"They'd have . . . " Larry began explaining.

"You don't have to spell it out for me," sighed Chris. "Gunshot'd be a dead giveaway. They'd know you're around and Whit's life wouldn't be worth a lead dime. If they didn't shoot him, they'd shield behind him." Now she pleaded. "Look, I know you're gonna have to play this careful, but d'you have to leave me here? Let me help. Loan me a rifle. Think I can't handle a Winchester? Listen, I can . . ."

"I'll leave mine with you, Red, 'case we get unlucky and you got to protect yourself," Stretch told her. "But here's where you stay, savvy?"

"We appreciate the offer." Larry showed her an amiable grin. "You're okay, Red. You're smart and you think fast, but Midas Mound's no place for you till we settle our business with Blystone and his men."

"Hey, I got business to settle too," she declared.

"Stay put," ordered Larry. "*We'll* take care of it."

The trouble-shooters unsheathed their Winchesters. Stretch passed his to the redhead, assuring Larry,

"I'll do good enough with my hoglegs."

"Bueno." Larry drew his Colt, checked its loading, reholstered it and took up his rifle. "Go ahead, beanpole. Say it."

"Here we go again," grinned Stretch.

They nodded encouragingly to Chris and moved north into the screening brush to begin their advance, leaving her to fume in resentment. Sanders was on her mind. She was in no doubt the Texans would size up the situation, time their moves with care and make their every shot count but, when the showdown began, what would be Whit's chances of survival?

"Got to try," she decided. "If I hang back, they won't know I'm comin'." She rose and, about to move off, paused to frown at the pinto and Larry's heaped gear. Rope. Those lariats might well prove useful. "Well, no big load to carry."

She helped herself to the coiled lariats, hooked them to a shoulder and, hefting Stretch's rifle, started for the brush.

Reaching the north rim of the brush, the troubleshooters dropped to half-kneeling positions and checked the set-up.

8

Cold Nerves and Hot Lead

WHAT the Texans saw warned them their strategy had better work and would have to be decided quickly.

Arno and Rolfe were getting to their feet, still with their Colts levelled at the two squatting prisoners. Blystone and the woman were emerging from the saloon, Rossiter, Mallick, McGrail and Elkin loitering by the horses. As his leader appeared, Arno grinned in anticipation and retreated a distance to lounge by the front of the building north of the saloon.

"What d'you say, Jarv?" drawled Rolfe. "All it takes is a couple bullets. I blast these losers now, we haul their carcasses to the creek and throw 'em in and that's that."

229

"Their bodies would be found eventually," countered Blystone. "And you can forget about shooting them. Sound of a shot carries a long way and we can't be certain the deputy's not already on his way here."

"So we knife 'em," suggested Mallick, shrugging callously.

"I have a better idea," grinned Blystone.

Nudging Larry, Stretch whispered,

"Ain't like a preacher now, Huh?"

"Sonofabitch faker," scowled Larry.

"What better idea?" demanded the woman.

"Their bodies will never be found," said Blystone, and he chuckled as he caught Wilkie's eye and gestured to the centre shaft. "Their deaths will be the result of a most unfortunate accident. They foolishly ventured into that shaft, part of which has already caved in. Once inside, the rest of it collapsed on them."

"No!" wailed Wilkie.

Something in Sanders, stubbornness

maybe, compelled him to show no fear. He eyed Blystone in contempt.

"You'll enjoy this," he accused. "You know what that makes you? By posing as a man of the cloth, you're already a hypocrite and a blasphemer. Now you're a sadist. And they don't come much lower than that, Blystone."

"Oh, Lord!" gasped Wilkie. "They mean to bury us alive!"

"Damn you, Wilkie, don't give them the pleasure of hearing you whine!" Sanders chided him.

"How'll we do it, Jarv?" asked Rolfe.

"It'll be easy." Blystone was still chuckling. "You prod them into the shaft, then we throw a few rocks. It'll be that simple. The clatter, the vibration . . . " He paused a moment, seeing death in the stare aimed at him by Sanders. Then he shrugged impatiently. "Get on with it. Get 'em in there."

"Well," Stretch said softly. "I don't guess we're gonna let this happen."

"Not so you'd blame well notice,"

muttered Larry. "Best we split up. You work your way around left of here, get to the mound and stake out. I'll sneak around the right side. Maybe I can cool one of 'em quiet, shave the odds a little, before the shootin' starts."

"All the luck, runt."

"You too. Tread wary now."

They separated as Rolfe ordered the captives to their feet and pointed them to the shaft. Wilkie was blubbering, his legs buckling; Sanders had to support him. All eyes were on them, otherwise some member of the band might have glimpsed Larry, who had crept, bent double, to the rear of the saloon and was turning its corner.

At the forward end, he saw Arno, his Colt holstered, watching the action. His back was turned and, so stealthily did Larry advance on him, there was never a danger he'd be alerted. Getting directly behind him, Larry gave him the butt of his Winchester, then grasped his collar with his free hand and dragged him backward. As he did so, he heard

Blystone's order to Rossiter.

"We'll be leaving soon as this is done. My grip's in the shack I shared with Verna. Go fetch it, Caleb."

"All the cash in it?" demanded Rossiter.

"Every dollar we took from the Quimera bank," Blystone assured him.

Larry emptied Arno's holster and let him drop, rammed the outlaw's pistol into his waistband and retreated to move north, keeping pace with Rossiter, glimpsing him as he passed the narrow passages between the shacks.

Hearing Rossiter's clumping boots in the third shack along, he turned its rear corner and made for its entrance. From the forward corner, he took a chance and thrust his head around for a quick scan of the ugly scene being played out. With guns at his back, Sanders had no option but to half-carry Wilkie into the centre shaft, the death-trap. Blystone and the woman were watching. He glimpsed his partner too, unnoticed by the outlaws, just his head and shoulders and gun-filled hands visible atop the mound. Nobody looking northward — so he must act *now*!

He sidled along to the doorway, then dashed in, gripping his rifle by its muzzle. Rossiter, in the act of picking up a valise, dropped it and, with his mouth opening for a warning yell, reached to his holster. Larry lunged at him, swinging the Winchester like a baseball bat fast and hard. The butt caught Rossiter's jaw, spinning him; he was as unconscious as Arno and his jaw fractured before he pitched to the floor.

Larry hauled the valise to the doorway, darted another glance south, discarded his rifle and, with his jack-knife, stabbed and ripped at the valise, tearing an eight-inch gash. He parted the gash long enough to satisfy himself as to what was packed into the grip. Paper cash, a lot of it.

Staring south, he saw McGrail throw a rock into the shaft. McGrail then bent to pick up another, a bigger one, and Stretch could wait no longer. His righthand Colt roared. The .45 slug ricocheted off the rock and McGrail dropped it as though it were red hot and whipped out his Colt and Stretch promptly fired again. As McGrail lurched with his chest bloody, Blystone and the others opened fire, forcing Stretch to duck. It was time for Larry to announce himself.

"Don't forget me, you sonsabitches!" he bellowed above the racket of gunshots. "I'm right here — where your loot is!"

As Elkin whirled to snap a shot at Larry, Mallick darted toward the saloon hefting his rifle. Cursing luridly, he ran along the side of the building to begin working his way north to the shack manned by Larry.

Elkin and Rolfe made the fatal mistake of charging the doorway where Larry crouched, only one thought triggering this impulse — he was there and so was the bank cash.

Their guns were roaring and, as a bullet sped past the brim of his Stetson, Larry levelled his cocked Colt and fired, stopping Elkin's rush. As though he had suddenly struck an invisible wall, Elkin jerked to a halt and began crumbling. Rolfe kept coming, running fast and taking aim, only to suffer the same fate. Again Larry's Colt boomed and Rolfe fell and writhed, pawing at his chest.

The rifle held by Blystone was torn from his grasp, struck by a well-aimed slug from Stretch's lefthand Colt. In a fury, Blystone turned and made for the pistol dropped by McGrail.

"Don't try it!" warned Stretch.

But now, though he had a clean bead on the boss-outlaw, he dared not squeeze trigger for fear of hitting a man he was here to rescue. There were ugly rumbling sounds from inside Shaft Number 2; the thunder of gunfire was having the expected effect. Sanders was emerging wild-eyed, dragging Wilkie by an arm. Once clear of the shafthead he thrust Wilkie aside and charged Blystone.

Just as Blystone's hand touched the fallen pistol, Sanders kicked savagely. Blystone took the swinging boot full in the face and was thrown backward, nose and mouth bleeding, and Sanders had only begun. He threw himself at the man who had condemned him to the death feared by all mining men while, from the shafthead, a cloud of dust spurted out. Then came the ugly clamor of the shaft collapsing, filling up, and Wilkie coughed frantically, crawled a distance and flopped with his face to the ground and his hands covering his head.

Sanders and Blystone were down and rolling, grappling, fists pounding, when Blystone's woman came edging toward them, pistol in hand. It was a bad moment for the taller Texan; Stretch had never in his eventful life shot at a woman. For him, it was a moment of anguish, but short-lived.

Another warrior was suddenly joining

the fray. In shock, Stretch saw a fire-haired fury rushing Verna, dropping rifle and lariats, ridding herself of his shirt for greater freedom of movement. The other woman saw her but, by then, Chris was in arms length.

"Hey, that's dirty fightin'," Stretch was moved to comment.

Chris's method of disarming Verna was effective, also drastic. She got both hands to the other woman's right wrist, forced the muzzle of the pistol away from herself and the struggling men and bit hard into the hand gripping it. Verna shrieked, let go of the pistol and struck at near-naked Chris with her other hand. Chris retaliated with a kick to the shin, after which they grappled, lurched off-balance and went down in a welter of threshing limbs.

Though distracted by what he could see from his vantage-point, Larry didn't fail to catch the warning sound somewhere behind him. Through an opening between planks of the rear wall the muzzle of a rifle had been thrust. He dropped flat the instant before the weapon barked and the slug cut through space just vacated by his torso. He rolled and, from his prone position, cocked and aimed his Colt. Now the rifle's barrel was dipping, the muzzle about to line on him again. He fired and, with his six-gun booming and jumping in his fist, recocked and triggered again and again. His first slug plowed through the plank wall three inches below the rifle's muzzle, his second and third some four inches above it. The rifle stayed wedged between the planks after he heard a cry of agony and the thud of a falling body.

He crawled through the doorway, rose and moved around to the back of the shack, tugging the commandeered Colt from his waistband. At once, he saw he would not need it. Groot Mallick was on his back, mouth and eyes wide open, his chest a mass of red.

A few moments later, he was hauling

the still unconscious Rossiter southward to where the battle was ending. Stretch was descending from the mound. Sanders was now straddling Blystone. Teeth bared, eyes dilated, he slammed at a wrecked face with both fists until Stretch arrived to grip his shoulder.

"He's out cold," he told the engineer. "You're wastin' your strength. Don't want to kill the skunk, do you? Leave him to the law, amigo. He'll hang for sure."

Sanders struggled upright and began the effort to regain control of himself. Then he, Stretch and the approaching Larry were gaping at the women. Red hair in disarray, her body and skimpy underwear streaked with dirt, Chris had gotten the better of her adversary. The woman called Verna was incapable of continuing their conflict when Chris lurched to her feet, hauled her to a half-upright position and swung her clenched fist to her face. Verna stiffened with her eyes glazing and went down flat on her back.

"Who was he?" sighed Stretch.

"Who was who?" challenged Larry.

"The first hombre that called 'em the weaker sex," said Stretch.

Larry had the answer.

"He was some fool that never met a gal like Red."

"Red, you were supposed to . . ." began Stretch.

"Hell, Red, don't you never follow orders?" demanded Larry.

She blew on her skinned knuckles and eyed him defiantly.

"Don't you bawl me out, Larry Valentine," she growled. "That no-good bitch was pointin' a pistol at Whit while he was beatin' up on her man, so it's lucky I *didn't* follow orders, okay? And I fetched your ropes along so you could hogtie any of these polecats you ain't already killed." In a somewhat belated attempt to regain her dignity, always assuming she cared two hoots for dignity, she marched back to where she had dropped Stretch's spare shirt and began covering herself. "And

241

now, if this hassle's all over . . . "

"It's all over, Red," grinned Larry. "And then some."

" . . . I'll go fetch some clean clothes and my soap," she finished, "and head back to the creek on account of I'm dirty all over and crave to get clean again."

As she moved past them, picking her way between the huddled bodies of the losers, Sanders addressed her formally, but with a wry grin.

"Of course you realize, Miss Christine Brodie, that having seen you in an almost naked condition, I'll have to marry you. Propriety must be observed, I insist."

She paused long enough to glance back at him and reply, "Fine by me, so long as you find us a genuine preacher, not another faker like Faber."

When she was out of earshot, the Texans eyed Sanders reproachfully.

"You'd better mean it," muttered Larry. "She's a helluva girl, Sanders, and she's had a lot of hurtin'."

"Don't fool with her," begged Stretch.

"I'm not fooling," Sanders fervently assured them. "I'm sure of how I feel about her because, when Mallick came back from chasing her and reported she'd drowned, I wasn't just shocked. I suddenly knew the meaning of grief, real grief. Her death would have been a loss to me." He followed the tall men as they moved to where Chris had dropped their lariats. "She called you Larry Valentine."

"That's my full handle," said Larry. "Familiar, huh? And how I wish it wasn't."

"So Woodville is actually Stretch Emerson," frowned Sanders. "Naturally I've heard of you and I should have guessed . . . " He snapped his fingers. "*That*'s why they accused you of theft. One of them must have recognized you and remembered your reputation. So you were potentially dangerous to them and . . . "

"That'd be right," nodded Stretch.

"About the gambler," said Sanders.

243

"He'd served a prison term and apparently Blystone was in the same prison. He had changed his appearance since then, but was afraid Arville would remember him."

"So it was Blystone knifed the tinhorn," guessed Larry.

"No," said Sanders. "Mallick. But Blystone gave the order. Valentine, I have a request. Please allow *me* to secure Blystone. I guarantee he'll not be able to free himself."

"Friend, I think you've earned that pleasure," declared Larry.

"How many others still livin', runt?" enquired Stretch.

"Just Blystone's woman and two I clobbered," said Larry. "Rossiter and a hard case in the alley by the saloon."

Wilbur Wilkie slowly rose, stared about dazedly, then trudged to the well. Sanders took pity on him and postponed hogtying the groaning Blystone long enough to work the windlass and draw a pail of water.

"What must you all think of me?"

sighed Wilkie, while dashing cold water into his face. "Pitiful sight — to say the least. How can I look any of you in the eye?"

As he set to work with Stretch's lariat, Sanders offered advice.

"Best forgotten. Try to put it all behind you, call it a harsh lesson and leave it at that."

"Easier said than done," muttered Wilkie.

"For past mistakes, we shouldn't punish ourselves the rest of our lives," said Sanders.

"You show me more kindness than I deserve," Wilkie said despondently.

A clip-clop of hooves announced the coming of a lone horseman. The Texans, busying themselves roping Rossiter and Arno, neither of whom showed signs of regaining consciousness, glanced northward, glimpsed the badge on the rider's vest and resumed their chore.

Deputy Covington rode in slowly, his jaw sagging. He hadn't viewed such a scene before — obviously. A red-haired woman shrouded in a man's shirt was walking southward from where he brought his mount to a halt, head held high, clothing and a towel draped over an arm. Three bloodstained figures lay in the grotesque postures of sudden death. A dejected-looking man sat by the well. An unconscious woman was sprawled on her back. Three men, two of them uncommonly tall, were working with rope, tying the hands and feet of three in a battered condition.

He dismounted slowly.

"Hell's sakes!" he breathed. "Hell's sakes . . . !"

He repeated the exclamation several times, might have continued indefinitely but for Larry, who surmised, "You'll be the deputy from San Raphael — here to tell us the pass is clear?" Covington nodded; he was still wide-eyed. "Fine, son. You might's well make yourself useful." He pointed to what had been Blystone and the woman's accommodation. "You'll find another stiff behind that shack. Inside you'll find a valise full of greenbacks which is the loot from a bank robbery at Quimera. You hearin' me clear? You look shook."

"What . . . " Covington swallowed a lump in his throat and licked his lips. "What — in blue blazes — *happened* here?"

"You know," Stretch remarked to Larry, "I *knew* that's exactly what he'd ask."

"Two things I'll tell you for starters, Deputy, just to get you breathin' and movin' again," said Larry. "Ever hear of the No Name Gang? This is what's left of 'em."

"Holy Moses!" gasped Covington.

"Ever hear of Valentine and Emerson?" challenged Larry. "This is Emerson, I'm Valentine."

"Holy Moses!" repeated Covington.

"Deputy," said Sanders, as he finished his chore. "Has anybody ever told you your vocabulary is monotonous?"

"That tin star gives you a right to

be plenty curious," Larry conceded. "We'll give you all the answers you want, but let's save that till we're headed for the pass. We still got chores here. Plenty extra horses like you can see, and stiffs to be roped to 'em."

"One other thing," said Sanders. "That woman. Use your manacles."

"Hands behind her back," warned Stretch. "She was one of 'em, kid, and she's real bad medicine."

"By damn," said Covington, at last bestirring himself. "The No Name Gang — and the Texas Trouble-Shooters."

As well as a change of clothing — just as garish as her other attire — Chris was wearing a bruise or two, legacies of her battle with Blystone's mistress, when she returned from the creek, but Sanders thought her to be the most admirable of women. The bodies of Mallick, McGrail, Elkin and Rolfe were hung across horses. Blystone, Rossiter and Arno were secured to other animals, feet lashed to stirrups, hands to saddlehorns.

"Time to pack up and move out, Red," said Larry. "My partner's hitched the team. He'll be drivin'."

"While everybody's packin' their stuff . . . " began Stretch.

"Sure," nodded Larry. "I'll fetch our horses."

He hurried south through the brush and, by the time he reappeared, straddling the sorrel and leading his partner's animal, repacked bags had been secured to the coach roof and the travellers were ready to reboard.

Tying the pinto behind the vehicle, Larry assured Covington Stretch was more than capable of handling the team and suggested they share the chore of leading the laden and riderless horses by tie-ropes. Covington agreed and finally got around to relaying the warning given by Bart Hayworth.

"When we make the pass, slow 'em to a walk," he instructed Stretch. "Gang from Sun Flats cleared a path wide enough to drive the coach through and we'll be right behind you, but no hustling."

"Danger of another rockfall." Sanders nodding knowingly while helping Chris aboard. "Yes, slow and easy does it. I'm sure Stretch understands."

Blystone's woman was already inside and seated awkwardly, hands manacled behind her back, a dishevelled, defeated bawd sporting a black eye, minus a front tooth and grimly silent now. Last to board, Wilkie chose the window seat opposite hers, keeping space between them. Even before the coach began moving, with Larry, the deputy and the laden horses following, he was mumbling apologies.

"I'm ashamed of my cowardice and unworthy of your forgiveness, Miss Brodie. But a humble file clerk can still be a gentleman, so I beg your pardon for my rudeness as a gentleman should."

"Why'd you lie about yourself?" frowned Chris.

The pudgy man winced, slumped

lower in his seat and bowed his head. Gently, Sanders made him an offer.

"She rates an explanation. Will you permit me? I believe I can make her understand without causing you excessive humiliation."

"Is that possible?" sighed Wilkie.

"Let me try," said Sanders, taking Chris's hand. "Chris, my dear, you must have known many people who yearned for respect, who wanted to make a big impression."

"You mean wanted to seem better than they are?" she shrugged. "Sure, plenty. I've known dirt-poor cattlemen that claimed they owned miles and miles of graze and were running ten thousand head of prime cattle beef, and sportin' gents that claimed they were loaded when they were down to their last few dollars. And me too. Think I've never dreamed of doin' my act on a big stage in a big, high-class theatre back east? Well, we can all dream, can't we?"

"So surely you can sympathize with

Mister Wilkie," suggested Sanders. "After many years of mistakenly believing himself to be unimportant, he wanted, just once in his life, to live *his* dream and pretend to be his own employer, the founder of a great corporation."

"Well, didn't do any harm 'cept to himself, did he?" She flashed Wilkie a reassuring smile. "Hey, Wilbur, no hard feelin's. I ain't' — I am not — mad at you."

"Thank you, young lady," Wilkie acknowledged, but with his eyes on the engineer. "*Mistakenly* believing myself to be unimportant?"

"Reconsider your position — and your responsibility," urged Sanders. "Can big business, banks, insurance companies, shipping houses and corporations like Kolbe Enterprises function without keeping records, records attended by conscientious filing clerks? No work is without worth. It may be poorly paid, yes, but still necessary."

"I never thought of it that way," muttered Wilkie. "But I wish I had."

During the journey back to the stage trail and westward to the ascent to the pass, Larry recounted to Covington all that had transpired since the derouted passengers had arrived in the ghost town. The deputy drank it all in, staring ahead to the baggage lashed to the coach roof.

"And it's all in one of those valises," he reflected. "They never did get around to sharing it out, all that bank cash. So the bank'll get it back and now there's no more No Name Gang."

"I figure Blystone's woman'll end up in a territorial pen," said Larry. "Blystone and the two we took alive — gallows-bait for sure."

"For sure," nodded Covington. "They did a lot of taking, and some killing too."

Stretch, after the ascent, slowed the team to a walk and warily scanned the high-walled corridor they now entered. Rock and rubble was piled high along the base of the rockwalls. The section cleared was just wide enough to permit passage of the rig and team, Larry and the deputy following side by side, the other animals being led through in Indian file. He disciplined himself against raising his eyes to the heights, sensing he wouldn't like what he saw up there and should concentrate all his attention on his slow-moving three spans.

Not a soul in sight. They progressed half-way through and kept moving, maintaining the funeral pace. Inside the coach, Sanders assumed a confident air, held Chris's hand and nodded encouragingly to Wilkie. Behind the vehicle, the two riders held reins in one hand, tie-lines in the other and darted apprehensive glances upward.

"I'm sweating," the deputy said softly.

"You and me both," Larry just as softly assured him.

"Think it's safe for us to talk?"

"Soft like this, I guess so."

"You'll have to tell it all again."

"You mean to your boss?"

"Well, sure. Sheriff Lunceford'll need statements from everybody."

"So how about this? You tell him what I told you, and we'll let the folks all do their own talkin'."

"Sounds okay."

The tag animals also passed the half-way mark. Onward they moved, Larry trying to pretend he wasn't hearing small rocks slithering and bouncing down, thudding to left and right of them. He was beginning to wonder, quite seriously, whether or not he and Stretch had eaten their last meal, smoked their last cigarettes.

With the west gate of the pass dead ahead, Stretch fought back the impulse to increase speed. He didn't breathe a sigh of relief when, at last, he drove the coach clear of the high walls and saw the trail extending across safe terrain; with his partner, the deputy and prisoner still in there, it was too early for sighs of relief or jubilant whoops. He saw the Sun Flats men gathered forty yards ahead beside the trail, men, wagons and horses, a sizeable deputation, but silent.

Driving that forty yards, he rose and stared backward. *Now* he could heave that sigh of relief. They were out and clear, Larry, Covington, every laden and riderless animal.

He was about to stall the team where the mine-hands waited when he, they and the passengers heard the sullen rumbling. Larry and the deputy turned in their saddles to stare backward.

"We m-m-must l-live right . . . " faltered Covington.

"Ain't that the truth," Larry said fervently.

The sullen rumbling became a deafening roar.

"I wouldn't," advised Sanders, as Wilkie made to thrust his head out his window. "You could suffer a heart attack."

"Hallelujah!" breathed Chris.

"Yes," he nodded. "We're safe — by a matter of moments."

The din persisted for most of a

minute, after which Bart Hayworth trudged to the now stalled vehicle, patted one of the trembling team-horses and addressed Covington and the travellers; he spoke with grim satisfaction.

"Bad scare for you people, but that's an end to it. There's no Fortuna Pass any more so, like it or not, the Hamilton Line has to plan a new route."

"It's filled in, Mister Hayworth," the deputy said shakily. "I swear we came through slowly like you told me and everybody keeping quiet as they could."

"I shouldn't have let you try it," Hayworth reproached himself.

"Calculated risk would you say?" prodded Sanders. "The vibration factor?"

"The rig and team and young Covington riding escort seemed safe enough," said Hayworth. "Of course, when I sent him to fetch you, I didn't know there'd be two riders following and all those horses." He frowned at the laden animals. "What happened at Midas Mound anyway? Some kind of shooting spree?"

"Mister, you wouldn't guess the half of it," declared Chris.

"You'll hear all about it in town, Mister Hayworth, and it's for sure you'll read of it in the newspaper," said Covington. "Got no time to explain it now. These folks need to make San Raphael and Sheriff Lunceford'll be waiting for my report."

"Don't linger then, son," said Hayworth. "I'll take this bunch back to Sun Flats and . . . " He glanced up at Stretch, "you pass right by the relay station, keep the team moving and you could roll into San Raphael before sundown." Sensing Sanders had knowledge of such matters, he remarked to him, "One thing about this whole mess. We made a saving."

"On dynamite," guessed Sanders.

"Right," nodded Hayworth. "From the minute we got here, I knew we didn't dare set charges. Every stick we brought along, every cap and coil of fuse, we'll be taking it back with us."

Stretch clucked to the team. The westbound rolled on with the escorts and horses following. And Wilbur Wilkie found his voice again.

"I scare easily," he admitted to Sanders and the redhead. "But I hope you agree I had ample cause — on this occasion. Dear Lord, after all we suffered at that ghost town, we could have been killed coming through the pass."

"I *do* agree," Sanders assured him.

"Too close for comfort," sighed Chris.

"It's an omen, a sign, if you care to look at it that way," mused Sanders. "We've been granted a reprieve." He stared hard at the other woman. "Well, not all of us."

The arrival of the last coach to be driven through Fortuna Pass was an event the citizens of San Raphael would long remember. It had been assumed the westbound would roll in eventually. What nobody, including Sheriff Earl Lunceford and the editor of the local newspaper, had assumed was that the coach would be driven in by a notorious trouble-shooter and that his equally notorious sidekick would be helping a deputy sheriff deliver eight prisoners, some dead, some in such pain that they probably wished they too were dead.

After listening to part of what Covington had to tell him, the scrawny sheriff ruled against having the passengers and the Texans crowd his office to have their statements recorded.

"You people must be mighty hungry, so let's do this the easy way," he decided. "I'll fetch a JP to the Cortez Hotel and you can answer my questions over supper or afterward."

The dead men were removed to a local funeral parlor, the wounded installed in the county jail, the woman Verna confined to a hotel room under guard and one of the San Raphael bankers summoned to take

260

charge of the recovered loot. One of Lunceford's deputies wired Sheriff Winters at Quimera, and a doctor was sent for to attend Blystone and his surviving henchmen in their cells.

Before supper, Sanders and Wilkie went to the Western Union office to telegraph explanations. The Simmons & Cole company was assured the engineer would arrive only two days later than expected. Wilkie's wire to his immediate superior in Los Angeles was wordier and sent collect; he felt entitled to explain that several life-threatening crises had caused his delayed return to duty. And it was his intention to present Kolbe Enterprises with a copy of the San Raphael paper's special edition to verify his claim.

While the now weary travellers worked on their first normal supper since quitting Quimera, they answered the sheriff's questions, the Texans adding their own versions so that, by the time the meal ended, Lunceford and the editor of the San Raphael

Leader knew all there was to know of the battle of Midas Mound and the defeat of the No Name Gang. The newspaperman demanded a follow-up interview with the trouble-shooters, who invited him to go chase himself.

An exhausted Wilbur Wilkie retired right after signing his statement. Sanders and Chris lingered over refills of coffee, she asking if his proposal had been a spur of the moment joke.

"I'm not holdin' you to it," she told him. "We're a whole lot different, you and me, and a gent like you could do better for himself. I know that, because one thing I never do is try to fool myself or make-believe I'm better'n I am."

"It was a time for joking," he muttered. "All that tension and the danger — culminating in your knocking Blystone's woman senseless. The blessed relief of humour, Chris. But my wanting to marry you was no joke. I'm serious."

"How serious?" she demanded.

"Let me put it this way," he said. "Our next stop is Tyson's Bend across the border. I'm told we'll make an overnight stop there and reach Vargas noon of the following day. Now I'm going to suggest you accompany me at least as far as Tyson's Bend and, when we get there, you'll have two choices. You can try finding work in a saloon while I check into a hotel room, or we can get married and check into the *same* hotel room."

She smiled wistfully and asked, "How much time do I get for makin' up my mind?"

"How much time do you need?" he countered.

"Well," she said, "I guess I could decide by the time we reach Tyson's Bend."

"That's soon enough," he grinned.

With all his paper work up to date, other law authorities advised of the demise of the No Name Gang and the Quimera bank cash in safe custody, Sheriff Lunceford expressed the opinion he should buy a drink for the outlaw-fighters whose reputation he knew so well. The invitation was worded somewhat formally and both drifters got the impression this lawman disapproved of trouble-shooters. Still, as long as he was buying . . .

Lunceford chose to conduct them to one of San Raphael's smaller bars, a hole-in-the-wall place on a side street. There he bought a bottle of respectable rye, asked for three glasses and led them to a corner table. They seated themselves. He pulled the cork and poured and, after their first mouthful had gone to where it would do the most good, conceded, "This isn't the first time you tumbleweeds have wiped out an owlhoot bunch. Like all the other times, it'd be fair to say you've done law and order quite a favour."

"Just one of those things, you know?" shrugged Larry. "We never even heard of the No Name Gang. We were just takin' it easy at Midas Mound and — uh — the stage arrived and things started happenin'."

"Nobody has to thank us," Stretch said modestly. "We just like to help out."

"Real nice attitude," approved Lunceford. "Still . . . " He sipped whiskey and warily appraised them, "I have to think of all the other hassles you jaspers mix into. Like, for instance, punching your way out of run-ins with proddy ranch-hands. You know the kind I mean. Hotheads with a hungering for glory, craving to be the brave fellers that beat hell out of the Lone Star Hellions. Trouble with such action is it almost always occurs in a saloon, and that can be destructive — windows smashed, furniture wrecked, stock damaged . . . "

"We've noticed that," nodded Larry.

"Next Saturday's payday for the cattle spreads hereabouts," remarked Lunceford. "Gonna be a lot of frisky cowhands riding in, hankering to kick up their heels and raise hell. Dodson Brothers're the three I'm thinking of.

Big fellers. A lot of muscle. They down a few shots of red-eye, they figure they can lick the world. Personally, I wouldn't give 'em one chance in ten thousand against you two. They'd likely end up in the county clinic in what the doctors call a reduced condition. Just thought I'd mention the Dodsons and — uh — ask how long you intend staying in San Raphael."

"Well, when a sheriff buys us a drink, we like to do right by him," drawled Stretch.

"Tomorrow mornin' we'd like to provision up and quit town," said Larry. "How does that sound to you?"

"It'd be a comfort to me and healthy for the Dodson brothers," said Lunceford.

"Suits us too," Stretch assured him. "On account of we're just a couple peace-lovin' hombres that don't like any kind of trouble."

"Sure you are," the sheriff said with a wry grin. "Sure you are."

*Books by Marshall Grover
in the Linford Western Library:*

BANDIT BAIT
EMERSON'S HIDEOUT
HEROES AND HELLERS
GHOST-WOMAN OF CASTILLO
THE DEVIL'S DOZEN
HELL IN HIGH COUNTRY
TEN FAST HORSES
SAVE A BULLET FOR KEEHOE
DANGER RODE DRAG
THE KILLERS WORE BLACK
REUNION IN SAN JOSE
CORMACK CAME BACK
RESCUE PARTY
KINCAID'S LAST RIDE
7 FOR BANNER PASS
THE HELLION BREED
THE TRUTH ABOUT SNAKE RIDGE
DEVIL'S DINERO
HARTIGAN
SHOTGUN SHARKEY
THE LOGANTOWN LOOTERS
THE SEVENTH GUILTY MAN
BULLET FOR A WIDOW

CALABOOSE EXPRESS
WHISKEY GULCH
THE ALIBI TRAIL
SIX GUILTY MEN
FORT DILLON
IN PURSUIT OF QUINCEY BUDD
HAMMER'S HORDE
TWO GENTLEMEN FROM TEXAS
HARRIGAN'S STAR
TURN THE KEY ON EMERSON
ROUGH ROUTE TO RODD COUNTY
SEVEN KILLERS EAST
DAKOTA DEATH-TRAP
GOLD, GUNS & THE GIRL
RUCKUS AT GILA WELLS
LEGEND OF COYOTE FORD
ONE HELL OF A SHOWDOWN
EMERSON'S HEX
SIX GUN WEDDING
THE GOLD MOVERS
WILD NIGHT IN WIDOW'S PEAK
THE TINHORN MURDER CASE
TERROR FOR SALE
HOSTAGE HUNTERS
WILD WIDOW OF WOLF CREEK
THE LAWMAN WORE BLACK

THE DUDE MUST DIE
WAIT FOR THE JUDGE
HOLD 'EM BACK!
WELLS FARGO DECOYS
WE RIDE FOR CIRCLE 6
THE CANNON MOUND GANG
5 BULLETS FOR JUDGE BLAKE
BEQUEST TO A TEXAN
THEY'LL HANG BILLY FOR SURE
SLOW WOLF AND DAN FOX

FIGHTING RAMROD
Charles N. Heckelmann

Most men would have cut their losses, but Frazer counted the bullets in his guns and said he'd soak the range in blood before he'd give up another inch of what was his.

LONE GUN
Eric Allen

Smoke Blackbird had been away too long. The Lequires had seized the Blackbird farm, forcing the Indians and settlers off, and no one seemed willing to fight! He had to fight alone.

THE THIRD RIDER
Barry Cord

Mel Rawlins wasn't going to let anything stand in his way. His father was murdered, his two brothers gone. Now Mel rode for vengeance.

ARIZONA DRIFTERS
W. C. Tuttle

When drifting Dutton and Lonnie Steelman decide to become partners they find that they have a common enemy in the formidable Thurston brothers.

TOMBSTONE
Matt Braun

Wells Fargo paid Luke Starbuck to outgun the silver-thieving stagecoach gang at Tombstone. Before long Luke can see the only thing bearing fruit in this eldorado will be the gallows tree.

HIGH BORDER RIDERS
Lee Floren

Buckshot McKee and Tortilla Joe cut the trail of a border tough who was running Mexican beef into Texas. They stopped the smuggler in his tracks.

BRETT RANDALL, GAMBLER
E. B. Mann

Larry Day had the choice of running away from the law or of assuming a dead man's place. No matter what he decided he was bound to end up dead.

THE GUNSHARP
William R. Cox

The Eggerleys weren't very smart. They trained their sights on Will Carney and Arizona's biggest blood bath began.

THE DEPUTY OF SAN RIANO
Lawrence A. Keating and
Al. P. Nelson

When a man fell dead from his horse, Ed Grant was spotted riding away from the scene. The deputy sheriff rode out after him and came up against everything from gunfire to dynamite.

FARGO: MASSACRE RIVER
John Benteen

The ambushers up ahead had now blocked the road. Fargo's convoy was a jumble, a perfect target for the insurgents' weapons!

SUNDANCE: DEATH IN THE LAVA
John Benteen

The Modoc's captured the wagon train and its cargo of gold. But now the halfbreed they called Sundance was going after it . . .

HARSH RECKONING
Phil Ketchum

Five years of keeping himself alive in a brutal prison had made Brand tough and careless about who he gunned down . . .

FARGO: PANAMA GOLD
John Benteen

With foreign money behind him, Buckner was going to destroy the Panama Canal before it could be completed. Fargo's job was to stop Buckner.

FARGO:
THE SHARPSHOOTERS
John Benteen

The Canfield clan, thirty strong were raising hell in Texas. Fargo was tough enough to hold his own against the whole clan.

PISTOL LAW
Paul Evan Lehman

Lance Jones came back to Mustang for just one thing — revenge! Revenge on the people who had him thrown in jail.

HELL RIDERS
Steve Mensing

Wade Walker's kid brother, Duane, was locked up in the Silver City jail facing a rope at dawn. Wade was a ruthless outlaw, but he was smart, and he had vowed to have his brother out of jail before morning!

DESERT OF THE DAMNED
Nelson Nye

The law was after him for the murder of a marshal — a murder he didn't commit. Breen was after him for revenge — and Breen wouldn't stop at anything . . . blackmail, a frameup . . . or murder.

DAY OF THE COMANCHEROS
Steven C. Lawrence

Their very name struck terror into men's hearts — the Comancheros, a savage army of cutthroats who swept across Texas, leaving behind a bloodstained trail of robbery and murder.

SUNDANCE: SILENT ENEMY
John Benteen

A lone crazed Cheyenne was on a personal war path. They needed to pit one man against one crazed Indian. That man was Sundance.

LASSITER
Jack Slade

Lassiter wasn't the kind of man to listen to reason. Cross him once and he'll hold a grudge for years to come — if he let you live that long.

LAST STAGE TO GOMORRAH
Barry Cord

Jeff Carter, tough ex-riverboat gambler, now had himself a horse ranch that kept him free from gunfights and card games. Until Sturvesant of Wells Fargo showed up.

McALLISTER ON THE COMANCHE CROSSING
Matt Chisholm

The Comanche, McAllister owes them a life — and the trail is soaked with the blood of the men who had tried to outrun them before.

QUICK-TRIGGER COUNTRY
Clem Colt

Turkey Red hooked up with Curly Bill Graham's outlaw crew. But wholesale murder was out of Turk's line, so when range war flared he bucked the whole border gang alone . . .

CAMPAIGNING
Jim Miller

Ambushed on the Santa Fe trail, Sean Callahan is saved by two Indian strangers. But there'll be more lead and arrows flying before the band join Kit Carson against the Comanches.

GUNSLINGER'S RANGE
Jackson Cole

Three escaped convicts are out for revenge. They won't rest until they put a bullet through the head of the dirty snake who locked them behind bars.

RUSTLER'S TRAIL
Lee Floren

Jim Carlin knew he would have to stand up and fight because he had staked his claim right in the middle of Big Ike Outland's best grass.

THE TRUTH ABOUT SNAKE RIDGE
Marshall Grover

The troubleshooters came to San Cristobal to help the needy. For Larry and Stretch the turmoil began with a brawl and then an ambush.

WOLF DOG RANGE
Lee Floren

Will Ardery would stop at nothing, unless something stopped him first — like a bullet from Pete Manly's gun.

DEVIL'S DINERO
Marshall Grover

Plagued by remorse, a rich old reprobate hired the Texas Trouble-shooters to deliver a fortune in greenbacks to each of his victims.

GUNS OF FURY
Ernest Haycox

Dane Starr, alias Dan Smith, wanted to close the door on his past and hang up his guns, but people wouldn't let him.

DONOVAN
Elmer Kelton

Donovan was supposed to be dead. Uncle Joe Vickers had fired off both barrels of a shotgun into the vicious outlaw's face as he was escaping from jail. Now Uncle Joe had been shot — in just the same way.

CODE OF THE GUN
Gordon D. Shirreffs

MacLean came riding home, with saddle tramp written all over him, but sewn in his shirt-lining was an Arizona Ranger's star.

GAMBLER'S GUN LUCK
Brett Austen

Gamblers seldom live long. Parker was a hell of a gambler. It was his life — or his death . . .

ORPHAN'S PREFERRED
Jim Miller

Sean Callahan answers the call of the Pony Express and fights Indians and outlaws to get the mail through.

DAY OF THE BUZZARD
T. V. Olsen

All Val Penmark cared about was getting the men who killed his wife.

THE MANHUNTER
Gordon D. Shirreffs

Lee Kershaw knew that every Rurale in the territory was on the lookout for him. But the offer of $5,000 in gold to find five small pieces of leather was too good to turn down.